# MY BROTHER PLATO

George Myerson

ANDERSEN PRESS

First published in 2024 by
Andersen Press Limited
20 Vauxhall Bridge Road, London SW1V 2SA, UK
Vijverlaan 48, 3062 HL Rotterdam, Nederland
www.andersenpress.co.uk

2 4 6 8 10 9 7 5 3 1

British Library Cataloguing in Publication Data available.

ISBN 978 1 83913 384 8

Printed and bound in Great Britain by Clays Ltd, Elcograf S.p.A.

*For Yvonne, Si and Elly,*
*with my love*

# PART 1

# LIES
# AND THE
# LAW

# One

My name is Potone, I'm eight years old and I live in the Greek city of Athens with my mum, my stepdad and my incredibly annoying little brother, Plato. I sometimes worry I must have been born on the fourth day of a new moon. If you are, it's really unlucky and that would explain A LOT.

There's a long war going on between Athens and Sparta, another part of Greece. We've been fighting with them since before I was born. I still don't really know *why*, though, because in other wars we've even been on the same side.

My mum has told me lots of stories about the Trojan war which happened a really long time ago. A big army from all of Greece went and sat outside this city called Troy for ten years – and the point is, the soldiers in this army came from Athens *and* from Sparta, as well as all over Greece. I don't see why we have to be enemies at all, when we used to be friends. When I say this, Mum smiles to herself as if there's something I don't understand about the world.

I want to start by telling you about the first time that long war came really close to me, right through our door and into my home. It was a couple of years ago now, so I was quite little still and my brother Plato, who is a year younger than me, was even smaller.

Our stepdad had gone with the army to fight against the Spartans. He was already quite old but all the men had to go because there was going to be such a big battle. The Spartans were winning the war then and they and their friends were attacking a great city over the sea called Delium. Athens had decided to send everyone we could to try and defend it.

The plan didn't work. Our men had to retreat and a few days after that, messengers reached the city saying our ships were going to arrive in the harbour later in the day. Mum was hoping Dad would be back that evening and praying that he would be all right. We had had no news of him.

My mum is tall with straight brown hair, like

mine, only longer and always tidy. She's also got these amazing, beautiful hands, with long fingers. Her fingers dance together to some tune inside them. She even walks as if she's keeping time to very soft music played on a harp no one else can hear. That day, she was moving in a very slow dance around the courtyard and then the house, where she was making sure everything was ready.

She was having a difficult time. This was partly because Plato and I were in the middle of one of our squabbling times – to be honest we have quite a lot of them! He had eaten all the figs we were meant to share for breakfast. I had told him it wasn't fair and this began an argument that went on for the rest of the day – it was now afternoon.

'It's not *unfair*,' was his first reply. 'I mean, you may not like it, but what's *unfair* about it?'

That's typical of Plato. He always picks on the words I use and twists them all around. Then I have to try and put him right. 'Fair is when everyone feels they've got what they ought to,' I answered. 'And I don't!'

That just started him off again. 'But I think *I* got exactly what I ought to!'

'Well, then you're *wrong* as usual!' I shot back

and before I knew it, we had left the figs behind and were arguing about everything else in the whole world! Mum had been trying to stop us for ages, but she couldn't.

Then, as if that wasn't enough for her, there was our big brother Demos. He's grown-up now and has his own house but he was still young enough to live with us then. Demos has been another big problem in my life too. The thing is, Dad is our second dad. When we were very small, we lived with our first dad, Ariston, and our mum who's called Perictione, in a big house in Collytus, a nice area full of trees on the edge of the city. But our first father died of the sickness which was spreading around the whole of Athens. After a while, Mum married Pyrilampes, who's our second dad – and came to live in an even bigger house in another part of Collytus. Demos was already here – he was Dad's son with his first wife who had died. He didn't seem very pleased when we arrived – and he always picked on us, whenever he saw a chance.

I was scared of Demos as soon as I saw him, with his long brown hair and angry eyes and I haven't ever got less scared.

That day, he kept on fighting with Mum about

everything she was doing to get the house ready. It was as if our home had its own little war, inside the bigger one between the city and Sparta. She had Dad's favourite vase moved into the hall, and he sent it back into the kitchen; she opened the shutters to let the breeze in, and he immediately shouted for them to be closed. Mum was doing her best to ignore him, and just get on – but that wasn't helping. In fact, I think her calm was only making Demos more annoyed.

'It is for *me* to decide how things should be here!' he yelled at her, after she had the vase brought back again. Then suddenly his eyes got this angry stare that I knew too well. Without any warning, he whisked the shiny stick he always carries and knocked the vase over so it fell with a crash and smashed on the tiles. Just for a moment, I thought Mum was going to cry. I heard her take a breath like a sudden gust of wind, and I could see her eyes begin to fill – but then she caught hold of herself and just called for the mess to be taken away.

'Please could someone . . . thank you!' she said, as if it was just one of those little accidents that always happen and is nobody's fault. Demos glared around. I saw his fingers tighten again on the handle of the stick and then he caught my eye. I looked away. I was determined that he shouldn't see any sign of the fear making my heart pump and pump so loud I thought it must be filling the room like a drum. Next to me, Plato moved forward but I stopped him with my arm – fighting was what Demos wanted! And it was obvious who would win!

The fear of Demos got all mixed in with the worry of waiting for Dad to come back.

I will always remember what happened next. Mum was coming down the stairs from arranging their bedroom with the slaves. The kitchen slaves were clattering as they got dinner ready. Then there was a hammering at the door. I can still see her standing in her best white robe with the green embroidery around the edge. For a moment, the dance of her feet and fingers stopped.

One of the slaves opened the big wooden door. And there was Dad. But he didn't walk into his home as he had left it. Two men were standing, one on either side of him, and he had his arms round their shoulders. He had his thick black cloak tightly wrapped about him. Slowly, they helped him into the house, one step at a time. He could hardly make it inside, even so.

Dad's a big man with a dark beard and bushy eyebrows. Just then, though, he looked as if he had shrunk. He hasn't got much hair left on his head and his face always has these crinkly lines all over it – in that moment they seemed to have got deeper, like the furrows in a field.

The only other time I had been so scared was when my first father was lying upstairs in our first home and even though I was so young, I knew he was about to die. Well, you tell me, if I *wasn't* born on the fourth day after a new moon, then why else do these things keep happening to me?

Dad's thick-soled sandals clunked on the tiles of the floor until he sank onto the first chair he came to. I felt *sure* he was dying too. His face was as pale as pure marble. He sat quite still, except for his hands, which shook as he clasped the sides of the seat. His eyes are dark, but that day they seemed this really deep black, like you could see right through into a strange night-time behind them.

The two men who had helped him went to the kitchen for a drink. Dad didn't move. Then I noticed that he had a cloth tied round his right leg. It must have been white once, but it was stained red from a wound underneath.

I looked up at Mum. She was standing with her hand on Plato's head. None of us could speak. She signalled to the slaves, and they went and fetched a big bronze basin of water from the washing room. I heard the water slopping as they came back.

She moved towards Dad. But then Demos, who had been as quiet as the rest of us, began shouting again, louder than I had ever heard anyone shout before.

'Leave *my* father alone! It is for me to take care of this! Women should have nothing to do with it – stand out of the way at once!'

Mum didn't reply, but she didn't do what he said either. While she unwrapped the cloth, Dad gave a groan that I can still hear. It seemed to come from far down a deep cave full of echoes, maybe even from the place buried under the earth that they call Hades, where people go after they die. I wondered if his spirit was already down there, making this moaning noise while his body was still up here on earth with us.

That groan was the first sound he had made. Immediately, Mum and Plato both started to cry. I was much too scared for crying. Demos had gone quiet again too – he didn't try to stop Mum any more. I could see his knuckles going white on the hand that held the stick. Then he gave one sudden bellow, as if he were talking to a huge crowd of people, though really it was only to himself: 'Revenge! We will be revenged on Sparta! They will pay for this with a thousand lives!'

He stopped and was silent again, but his anger seemed to fill the house, like the heat of a fire.

Meanwhile, Mum made sure they carried Dad upstairs to his bed. Demos stood watching until, with one more glare of rage at me and Plato, he turned and stormed up to his rooms without another word. The only sound now was our dad's soft moaning and the gentle words of Mum as she tried to get him settled. Even Plato and I couldn't keep up our argument and so the rest of the evening was one of the quietest I have known.

That was the day the big war in the world came into my home and got mixed with the little wars in the family, between Demos and us and between me and Plato. I am going to tell you about all of these wars – and how they have got churned up together to make my life. But my story is also about trying to make peace.

# TWO

At first, we all thought Dad would never walk again. He lay in bed for many days, until he began at last to hobble about with a stick. I could hear it thumping on the floor of the bedroom. After that, he limped down the stairs and sat in the sun in the courtyard. And now he can walk wherever he wants, except a bit like he is on the deck of a ship in the wind.

As soon as he could, he started to go out to meetings of the Assembly again. He had to. Dad is a very important man in Athens. He's friends with the most powerful citizens. Years ago, he used to be what they call an 'Ambassador' for Athens to Persia, a huge country that was our enemy. He spent a lot of time living there and talking to their king. Eventually they did end the war between us. Even if now there's war with Sparta instead!

When there was peace, he came home to Athens with many leaving gifts, because everyone was so pleased to be friends. There's a Persian robe with lots of colours woven into it. We also have a beautiful bowl made of gold in our house that was a present to him from their king. It shines like the sun. But the best thing the Persians gave him are some strange birds that no one else has in the whole of our city. They're famous in Athens and they're called peacocks. What's odd is that they've got feathers and wings but they don't like to fly! Instead, these peacock birds walk around nicely on long thin legs. The amazing thing about them is they have tails that can spread out like the sails of a ship behind them. I used to think the blue speckles on these big tail feathers were lots of eyes looking at me!

When my brother and I first came to live in this house, the peacocks were as tall as me, and towered over Plato. While I was quite scared of them, he used to get into trouble for chasing them around the courtyard. Well, he still does sometimes, even now we're bigger! They can move pretty fast, which surprised me when I first saw them run.

He'll never catch them really – and I don't know

what he would do if he did. I sometimes tell him he's just chasing the wind with a net – that's one of my favourite old sayings that I keep in my mind and bring out to make me feel better – and to irritate Plato. The wind just blows through the holes in your net, of course, so it means doing something that is completely impossible. The picture it gives makes me smile, like a lot of the sayings, even when the meaning is a bit sad.

A sad saying makes me calmer because I feel less alone. I always think there must be lots of other people who have had the same troubles, for those words to be something people say and remember.

Plato doesn't like my sayings! He says he's not trying to catch the peacocks really, so he's not chasing any wind with a net, just running round and round to give the birds some exercise. But I can tell he'd like to grab one if he could!

Sometimes Dad comes out into the courtyard to tell my brother to stop chasing his birds. He's got a very deep voice, but actually he doesn't like to shout. Even when he's telling Plato not to bother the peacocks, he talks quite gently. Still, you can tell he's used to lots of people doing as he says. He just looks and sounds like he expects to be obeyed. In fact, I'd say my brother is the only one who *doesn't* take much notice!

Anyway, I've told you about the Persian peacocks because they were a really big part of the next time *big* trouble came rushing into my life!

# Three

The day of that next really huge problem started out totally ordinary. Plato had to go to school. That's never my favourite thing, because as a girl *I'm* not allowed to go. I often feel frustrated and even angry when my brother sets off, with his school helper carrying all his scrolls and everything. I was really sad that morning.

I often think of the story about a poor farmer who finds a magic ring. He uses it so he can walk around without being seen – and that's what I wanted!

'If I had that magic ring, like poor Gyges found, you know what I would do with it, Dad?' I said.

'What would you do, Potone?' he replied softly.

'I would make myself invisible and go to school with Plato,' I answered. 'Mind you, I don't know why girls can't just go without any magic!'

Dad nodded and looked serious. 'Yes, I can see

that,' he said, looking down with a sad smile. 'But there's nothing even I can do about it.'

'The *Spartans* let their girls go to school, don't they?'

'That's true, they do,' he said after a short pause to think. 'But they're our enemies now, so it's hard to copy them. Maybe when the fighting is over, then we can learn from them. Yes, that would be a good thing!'

I didn't think that was really a proper answer. He was just trying his best to be kind. I felt inside me that wanting to go to school was like blowing against the wind – it was too strong, and my breath was lost in it.

Still I *was* learning reading and writing from my mum. We usually stay under the shade of the tree when it's hot, but that day was cool enough for us to sit in the open by the fountain. Life may be one great sea of troubles that we sail over, but it does have these little islands too, and that morning was a lovely green island with flowers and a gentle breeze.

Mum was telling me that, way back in her family, ages and ages before even her grandfather, there was a famous man called Solon. He wrote down the rules the people of Athens ought to follow, and how

17

to understand them. Solon called this 'The Tables of Law', which meant 'The Big List of Rules'. It is one of the most important books in all of Greek, Mum says. And since his time, *everyone* in the family has been taught to read and write, girls as well as boys – and she always says she has to make sure that's true for *me* as well, because otherwise how will I teach my daughters?

That morning, I wrote lots on my wax tablet with the metal stick. I really believe that written words can talk better than even the loudest of yelling voices! I know you can't hear what writing says out loud, unless you speak for it. But I think written words have their own very quiet speech, which sort of echoes in your head. Other people who loved writing and reading before me called the letters themselves 'silent wisdom'. It makes me feel part of this big group, all listening to the same words from long ago until today.

Mum had told me a story about a man called Odysseus. After the war with Troy, the Greeks all sailed home, but he had annoyed some of the gods, so they stopped his ship from getting back. Instead *his* journey took years and years, and he had so many adventures. All that time, his faithful dog, called Argus, waited for him. At last when Odysseus did get home, in disguise, the dog knew him. Argus welcomed his master home – and then died peacefully and happily. The dog was old, but he had been staying alive to be there for his master. I decided to write the story of Odysseus coming home, only this would be told by his dog, Argus!

Our *own* faithful dog, Tigris, was sitting near me, keeping an eye out for peacocks. He's not very sure about those big birds. They don't like him much either and often peck their beaks at him to make him go away. Most of the time they don't make any sound, except they do screech at Tigris and that scares him even more. He was staying under my bench and watching out, with his brown tail flopping from side to side.

There were no peacocks nearby today. It was so peaceful that it was hard to imagine war still going on between us and Sparta. Fighting stopped in the winters anyway, but as soon as spring came, and it was not far away now, the battles usually started again. I had heard Mum and Dad talking about it, even though they tried to stop me hearing. I knew that they were worried in case this year our enemies decided to attack Athens itself.

Then this little bubble of peace at home went *pop!* My brother came back from school with his school helper carrying all his stuff, writing things and reading things. I wished I had them too. As soon as he got home, he just sat right down in the courtyard and started complaining. He had spent a lot of the time writing too, but he hadn't enjoyed it like I had. In fact, he had come back really angry about the whole idea of writing. Of course, that started a big row.

This is how it went, like in a play:

**PLATO:** I would *ban* all writing! It's useless, just a waste of time . . .

**ME** (unable to wait till he's finished saying this!): What? No! Writing things down makes them something we can share. It's like a gift for lots of other people. I mean, there's a written story where Odysseus comes home and his dog Argus has waited for him for ten years – and it's only because it's written down that Mum was able to tell me about it, and now I've written my *own* story about what the dog Argus must have felt.

**PLATO** (interrupting back): I don't *need* writing to help me think of things. I have my own ideas in my head – and I bet I know more about real dogs than any old story can tell me!

*Here our own dog, poor Tigris, takes himself away, with a loud whine as he goes. He had been sitting peacefully by us – now our company is not worth the stress of hearing us quarrelling! I am sorry to see Tigris go, but I have to keep trying to put Plato right. If he doesn't like learning to write at school, I'd be glad to go instead of him!*

**ME:** That's all your usual salt and beans, Plato!

**PLATO:** What in Hades do you mean by that? I suppose it's another one of your stupid sayings!

**ME:** Salt and beans is what soothsayers pretend to use to tell the future – it's all rubbish and so is everything *you* just said!

**PLATO:** I *knew* it! Potone the Proverb! That's who you are! Why can't you just talk for yourself? Why keep repeating all that old stuff? I suppose that's more old writing instead of your own ideas!

**ME:** I *am* talking for myself – and I'm talking sense too, unlike you – all your ideas are getting tangled up like when I drop a ball of wool! It's obvious that ideas get wasted if they *don't* turn into writing.

**PLATO:** People like you think all those pages of words are keeping ideas safe. But really things die once someone writes them down – because nobody bothers to think about them once they're on one of those silly old pages.

**ME:** If you did write down what's in your head, at least the place would be a lot more peaceful than with you *arguing* with everyone!

**PLATO:** It's everyone else, like *you*, who argues with me; I don't argue with them. *I'm* only saying what I think. Well, at least I *do* think . . .

Now we were both getting really fed up. It was turning into an angry quarrel. There's an old saying that nobody annoys a man more than his brother. Well, that's true for us if you make it about brothers *and* sisters.

I do know that lots of people would think this was a fuss about nothing. I have a saying for that too! You could have said we were arguing about smoke. This picture kind of drifted into my mind, as I tried to calm down.

The trouble was, Plato's mistakes about writing were the most *annoying* of all the things he says, as I would love the lessons he hates.

And one argument always leads to others once we've got started. We couldn't stop it that day, even when we had gone inside and upstairs to the women and children's room. Our mother was already up there. This was usually a cosy time. Plato was still insisting that he knew more about dogs than I do, and that he didn't need any writing to help him understand Tigris and how clever our pet is. I knew he was just doing it to annoy me, but still I felt I couldn't just let him go on saying this kind of nonsense.

'Do you think you know more about dogs than all the people who have ever written about them?' I was almost crying, I was so fed up!

The symbol of our city is an owl. It's the favourite bird of our goddess Athena, so we're kind of famous for our owls. There are even owls on our coins. If someone wants to say you should stop doing the same thing over and over, they say you're sending owls to Athens, which of course has plenty of them already. Well, I think arguing with my little brother like that is really my way of sending more owls to Athens. He's got too many ideas of his own, there's no point in adding more, even if they *are* better than the ones he's got.

There were too many owls flapping around me and my brother altogether! But it was hard to stop.

The quarrel was getting messier. The room was full of crazy owls, ideas whizzing around everywhere.

'Can't you two *stop* that?' Mum was pleading.

Then suddenly we *did* stop arguing!

# Four

There was a terrific racket from the courtyard below.

'Down, crazy beast! Get *down* at once!'

We both knew who *that* was – it was Demos, back again like an old fire breaking out!

Next thing, there was a thumping noise, and then a loud howling and barking. Tigris! Of course we could tell he was hurt. The howls got higher and higher, as if our poor dog was screaming.

'That'll fix you!' came Demos's deep voice, even more fiercely. Then there was another heavy thump.

I was out of the door and running as fast as I could down the stairs, before anyone could stop me. Even as I was rushing along, I still heard a woman's calm voice in my head saying 'hurry slowly', which means you can go too fast, as well as too slow. In a way, it was true – perhaps what I did next actually made our troubles worse. There just *are* times when you have to stop thinking! I nodded a kind of sorry to the wise woman who gave me that warning, but I didn't slow down!

'Come back, Potone! Come back at once!' I heard Mum calling – too late. I wasn't going to wait. Tigris was whining now, between barks. *Whine . . . bark . . . whine . . . bark!* I could hear my feet skimming over the wooden steps as I charged down. Mum once told me about the god Hermes who has wings on his feet – well, I imagine them on his ankles really, but wherever they are, he runs like the wind. I was trying to run as fast as Hermes!

In another moment, I was out into the courtyard. There was enough daylight left to see clearly across the yard, where already the torches were burning along the walls. What I saw made me feel as if I had dropped the whole earth from my shoulders and it had fallen down and broken in pieces.

Demos was standing by the fountain. When we first knew him he was a thin boy with angry eyes, but he's grown into a tall strong man, with long hair and a thick curly beard. He was wearing a heavy black cloak, with golden thread that shone in the gloom. His right arm was lifting a stick, with a shiny metal tip like the one he had used to smash that vase while we were all waiting for Dad to come home. It caught the light from the flames around the walls.

In Athens we have a god of war, called Ares. He's always angry and keen to fight, which is scary enough. What's even worse is that he has two sons called Deimos and Phobos. They're the gods of fear, and it felt to me as if this Demos was a third god of fear, tramping into our quiet home. If *that's* not what such a god looks like, I don't know what is!

At his feet was our Tigris, crouched and howling. Demos's other hand was gripping the fur on his back, so he couldn't escape. The stick was about to come down again, and the barking got more and more frantic. Tigris could also tell what was coming next.

Before I knew it, I had run over and grabbed hold of my older brother's cloak. It felt like poking a lion, so close to real danger. I was full of panic, from the top of my head to the tips of my toes. It was tingling inside me.

Despite that, I carried on tugging for all I was worth. I was shocked at how strong I was! Demos was tall and broad, but he wasn't expecting to be clutched like that. He staggered sideways and as he tried to get his balance, he let go of the dog. We both toppled over and Tigris rushed away to the other side of the courtyard.

Right then, Plato came out, and our dog went over to him, shuffling and whining.

'Tigris! Poor little Tigris!' I could hear Plato saying in a comforting sing-song voice.

Already Demos was back on his feet, and I couldn't stop him now. He shrugged me off and all I could do was shriek: 'Help! Stop him! He'll kill Tigris!'

I saw the bronze tip of Demos's stick flashing as he ran towards my younger brother and Tigris. But he never reached them.

In plays, Mum tells me they have something called 'the god of the machine'. When everything in the story is terrible, and it seems like everything is lost, a god appears and solves the problem – and often they lift him up high on a kind of machine above the stage, which is where the name comes from. Even if there weren't any gods around to rescue us then, it did feel like that kind of moment.

'Get hold of him now!' said my dad in his quiet voice. Almost at once, two of our biggest slaves rushed across the courtyard and seized Demos.

He would have hit out with his stick if he had the chance, but they were too quick for him and too strong. The stick fell to the ground and they held him tight, their arms around his body so he couldn't move.

'What's all this hubbub?' Dad asked, as if he was trying to solve a puzzle, not talking to a wild man who was struggling to get free.

I rose to my feet and searched for a voice in my throat. I was sobbing in between my words. The story came tumbling out in bursts, until I ran out of breath: 'Dad ... he was attacking Tigris! He was hitting him with that ... that metal stick ... he would have killed him ... I'm *sure* he would have killed him! We heard Tigris howling from upstairs and I ran down ... and tried to stop it ...'

'*Look* at our dog, Dad!' Plato picked up the story and took over from me. 'You can see he's hurt! If Potone hadn't stopped him, that mad monster would have beaten Tigris to death!' Tigris was whining and panting as my brother stroked him.

'Tell your men to take their hands off of me!' Demos was yelling, while we were talking. 'I won't forget this outrage! I'll make sure all of the citizens know how you have treated *me*!'

'You may let him go, please, and thank you for acting so swiftly,' Dad told the two men, and they slowly relaxed their grip. Their eyes stayed fixed on Demos, as they stood by him in their plain white tunics. One of the men, with long brown hair and bright blue eyes, had the ghost of a smile when my stepfather thanked them. He bent down and picked up the stick, keeping it well away from Demos.

By now the evening had got dark. The torches shone more brightly around the courtyard, making strange shadows of us all on the walls of the house as we moved. If there really is a place called Hades, where the dead go, I think it couldn't look any spookier.

Demos spat each word in his rage: 'Let's see what the people of Athens have to say about you setting men on me as if I had broken in.' He was glaring right at me as he said those last horrible things. This was even more frightening because he was already quite important in the city. I knew he made lots of speeches, usually about winning the war and defeating the Spartans. Unlike Dad, who had spent so much time searching for peace, he was keener for us to keep fighting! There were plenty of people who liked what he said – and as I heard him,

I wondered if he could even lead a gang of them to attack our house if he got really angry!

I was as scared as I would have been if the god of war *was* rushing to attack me. I found myself stepping back out of the light into the safety of a dark corner of the courtyard.

'That will do!' Dad replied, as if he was saying something true, rather than giving a command. 'What made you think you could come into this house and start attacking our dog, let alone the kids?'

I saw Demos's shoulders moving and I was sure he was going to make a rush to get away. But the house men had also seen him stirring and they gently held his arms again. Now he started to talk in a new way, calmly, as if he were in a court, defending himself.

'I decided to visit my own home, which this house is, whatever *you* all think! I took a moment in the courtyard and while I was here, this foul-smelling hound dared to attack my noble peacocks.' He paused and changed his words, with a sneer in his voice: 'I mean, *your* noble peacocks ... in another second, he would have been biting them, I am certain of it. There would have been nothing but a heap of

31

feathers if I had not acted so quickly to stop him! Then, after I saved the birds, the cur turned on me instead and opened his jaws to bite me! It must be in his nature to hate everything as noble as I am!'

He stopped, as if he was thinking about what to say next. In the gap, I could hear Tigris still whining in pain. Demos carried on telling his story: 'In fact, he bit my leg before I managed to drive him off. I have never heard of such a wild beast being kept as a pet, not in any *proper* house!'

'That's what happened then?' Dad said quietly. 'You saved the peacocks from this wild dog, who then bit you?' I was sure this was exactly the way men would have talked in a proper court, after listening to him telling his story.

It was impossible to know whether my dad believed what Demos had said. He didn't give any hint in the way he spoke. This calm seemed to make my older brother catch fire again!

'You don't believe me, your own son! You stand there as if you were listening to a . . . a *foreigner* you didn't trust! I'll have justice, that's what I'll have! *Justice!*'

Demos shouted this word. He glared first at me and then at Plato, who was still cradling Tigris.

I was so afraid, I thought my heart would stop beating. What did he mean to do now?

Demos began to yell at Dad again.

'Your dog has bitten me and wounded me badly, when I was simply protecting my property. You yourself, my father, know perfectly well what the laws of Athens say about that. Solon made a law against such dangerous brutes. And I demand what that law says! I am going to take this dangerous wild dog away and have it put down . . . and if you don't give it to me, I'll bring my followers to help me seize it!' Here he turned to me. 'And they'll make sure *you* don't keep any more beasts like it again!'

This came out in a rush of words. It was hard for me to follow. I was so scared, I felt like a fawn that was trying to fight a lion. But I got the main idea. Demos wanted to take Tigris from us and have him killed! As I had imagined, he was threatening to bring a mob to help him. He also said that he was allowed to do this by Solon's law! Could any law truly let him do such a thing? Was that a *real* law?

Usually I can't speak when I get very scared. Now I found myself talking really fast.

'Dad! *Can* he do that? He can't, can he?' I asked. I was shocked to hear my own voice, as if it were

33

someone else talking from the other side of the courtyard. Since I was standing in shadow, I think my question came as a surprise to everyone else too.

Demos turned around again. 'You will *see* whether I can or not! I'm an important citizen and I know my rights! I won't let you bring your brute into this house to drive me out!'

All this time, poor Tigris was huddled on the ground, staying close to Plato. How could Demos call this fluffy friendly dog a brute and a monster? *I* was sure he was lying.

Dad hadn't answered my question about the law straight away. After a pause, he began to answer: 'Well, my dear, there *is* a law of Solon about dogs that bite, yes, that's true. This is a very old law which has been in the city a long time. It is carved with the oldest laws on the stone tablets near where the courts meet.' He spoke slowly and carefully, so each word was clear. Even Demos stopped trying to interrupt and waited in silence for him to finish. 'This law does say that a citizen who is bitten by a dog can take it away. In fact, the same law also says that the dog must be put in a big wooden collar when it is given up to him. And he may do as he pleases with the animal after that . . .'

Demos couldn't wait any longer now. He began yelling once more: 'That's *true*, you admit it! I demand my right to take this brute away *now*! I'll soon make sure he doesn't bite any other respectable citizens of Athens with those monstrous jaws! You won't be seeing *him* again!'

At these last words, he gave a kind of furious laugh. I couldn't bear it!

I had noticed Plato staring at Dad as he explained the law. Now he joined in, stroking the dog while he spoke: 'Dad, did you say a citizen may take away a dog that has bitten him, but it must be wearing one of these special wooden collars?' he asked.

'Well, yes,' replied Dad, turning to look at my brother crouched down with Tigris in the corner of the courtyard by the tree.

I realised at once what Plato meant. I had had a lot of practice at working out how his ideas grow.

I might be a fawn, but I tried dressing up in a lionskin and sounding as brave as I could: 'So . . . without that collar, the dog can't be taken away, Dad, isn't that true? And has this . . . has Demos got one of these wooden collars with him?' I had to stay calm and not sound scared or angry. That would have no effect on our dad. 'Does the law of Solon mean if there is no wooden collar, the dog must stay here?'

These questions were harder than anything I usually ask! He paused to think, and while he did, Demos, who wasn't interested in my questions or anyone else's either, just threw more words back at me and my younger brother: 'How dare you speak like that, you mangy brats! If the law was sensible, I would be allowed to take *you* and finish you off too, before you bring any more harm to my precious birds! They are priceless, and you're worth *nothing*!'

Demos really knew how to say things that hurt! I would usually have died with horror and shame if someone talked to me like he had. Instead I told myself, 'Don't listen to him, you're *not* nothing, you're *someone* just like him!' I was too worried about Tigris to give in. I wouldn't let a bully stop me talking.

'But isn't this true, Dad? The law of our ancestor Solon means he can't just take Tigris away now, can he? *Can* he?'

This time Dad answered quickly, before there was another outburst from his older son. 'Indeed, that *is* how it seems to me, my dears, I agree,' he said slowly, as if he was still weighing up the arguments on both sides. 'The law does say that such a dog must be taken away in a wooden collar, one that is exactly three arms in length to bind the dog and hold it by. Without that, I think the animal must stay where it is for now, yes.'

When he heard this, Demos tried to argue back. 'That's total rubbish! The collar is only to keep the brute from doing more harm, and I'll make sure he doesn't have a chance when I get my stick back!'

'I don't believe you can choose to have only one bit of a law without the rest of it,' Dad replied, shaking his head steadily and staring at the shadows flickering over the rough plaster walls. 'If you don't have a wooden collar three arms in length, then you *can't* take the dog away.'

I felt joy rising like a fountain! When the feeling reached my mouth, I had to laugh, I was so happy to hear he wasn't going to agree to Demos taking Tigris away. Dad carried on: 'Still the law is clear. If you return with such a collar, you may indeed take away a dog that has bitten you . . .'

The torchlight seemed to go dark as I heard these words, and the night went black as Demos replied with an angry grin, 'Then tomorrow morning I'll be back *with* the collar, and I can tell you it will be all the worse for the dog since I have had to wait!'

Here he took a step forwards and the house men started to lean towards him. Dad nodded to them and they let our grown-up brother walk across the courtyard and into the house. From there he stormed out into the street beyond – for now.

# Five

When Demos had gone, my brother and I both started to cry properly. Mum came out into the courtyard, and we ran over to her. I could feel her fingers dancing gently and comfortingly over my head. Plato was huddled on the other side of her – we had one hand each. While she touched our heads lightly and stroked us, just like my brother had stroked Tigris, Dad told her exactly what had happened. She knew that any trouble with Demos would get much worse if she came in, which is why she'd stayed out of the way until he went off.

'So, he thinks he has the law on his side, does he?' she said softly, as we tried to stop sobbing and listen. 'But *is* Solon's law so simple?'

Dad gave a little grunt as if he agreed that this was a good question. Meanwhile, Tigris was creeping over towards us and now he joined our huddle with

Mum. He was still making a kind of whining sigh with each breath.

Plato and I both stopped our tears. And of course, as soon as we were calmer, we started to think about what was going to happen.

'He'll be back with a collar tomorrow,' I began. 'He'll be getting it made for him tonight! *Better luck next time*, that's what he'll be thinking, won't he, Dad?'

Before Dad could reply, my brother got in ahead of him. Even now, he couldn't let a saying pass!

'I just knew you'd have one of your mouldy old sayings for this, Proverb girl!' he teased, but he didn't really sound annoyed now, because we were on the same side here – and anyway he could see it *was* what Demos would think!

Dad agreed: 'Better luck with the next roll of the dice, yes that's about right, Potone. Proverbs and sayings can be true – that's why people remember them!'

'Anyway, this law.' I got back to the big question. 'Dad, you said if a dog has bitten a citizen, the law is that he can take it away in a wooden collar and . . . and . . .'

'*If* a dog has bitten a citizen . . .' said Plato. 'But *has* our Tigris really done that?'

'That could be quite a big *if* couldn't it?' I said.

We both smiled. Everything was still scary, but we couldn't help smiling at each other! Now it was lucky we had spent so much of our time arguing to and fro! That helped us to think *together* when we needed to. We both knew exactly what the other one was going to say next, because that's exactly what you need to know if you're going to get better at answering back!

'We'll both have to try and make that *if* a big question, not just a little word!' came the squeaky voice that I was so used to arguing against.

'Yup, what we have to do is take that *if* and wake it up with all its eight feet!' I was talking quickly, like I usually do when I'm excited.

'Oh, what *are* you on about now?' my brother couldn't stop himself saying – I *knew* he'd be surprised by those eight feet. 'I suppose it's another of your stupid sayings, but just for now you'd better tell us what you mean!'

'What has eight feet then?' I had to tease him a little bit.

'Eight feet? Ummm, two dogs? Four people?' he answered, starting to get irritated.

'Nooo.' I wondered whether to keep him waiting a bit more, but then I thought we had to get on. 'It's a scorpion, you know they have eight legs, don't you? Well, they've also got the worst sting, haven't they? So, if you wake up a scorpion it's really dangerous – and that little word "if" will be as dangerous as any scorpion to Demos by the time we've woken it up!'

'Ohhh, yes,' said my brother, and for once he didn't make fun of me. 'Yes, that sounds good, a scorpion on our side is *definitely* what we need!'

Then I had another idea, as we stood there in the flickering courtyard.

'What else does the law say about dogs, Dad?' I asked.

'Yes, Dad, doesn't the law say anything about being *fair* to dogs?' Plato was quick to pick up ideas from me too. 'After all, dogs have feelings as well, don't they? You can tell they're thinking thoughts, can't you? So, don't we have to be fair to them, just like with people?'

'Hmm,' Dad said, as he pondered our questions. 'Nothing stays simple for long once the two of you start talking about it!' And he smiled, so I knew he didn't mean to tell us off for talking too much. He wanted us to be sure he was listening. 'But now we must go inside before we do any more thinking in the cold!'

Inside the house, we sat down again and carried on trying to solve this problem together, while we had our hot milk and bread. How *were* we going to stop Demos taking our dog away tomorrow when he came back with that wooden collar? I couldn't bear the idea of seeing Tigris crushed under that heavy weight and whining for us as he was dragged away by his enemy!

'Don't dogs count in the law?' asked my brother, picking up the last question from outside.

'Ah yes, you were just asking that.' Dad lowered his head and stroked his beard, like I am sure the President of the Council at a big trial would do while considering a tricky point in court. 'Well, my dear, I'll tell you one thing you might be surprised about. Let's say there's a big heavy statue standing on a wall. If it topples over and squashes someone going past, and no one pushed it over, then there can be a trial of the *statue* to decide if it is guilty of a crime! And if the citizens judging the case says it's guilty, they cast it out of the city. But if it is innocent, it gets put back where it was before. And that can be true of any other thing that might have harmed someone too.' I could tell even he was puzzling over this law as he spoke.

'But what about animals then, Dad?' I put in before he went on to another law.

'Yes, Dad, *surely*,' added my brother quickly, 'since a stupid dead statue has to have a fair trial, so does a real dog! I mean, it can't be the law for Tigris to be taken away for supposedly biting Demos without both sides being heard, can it?'

'Doesn't he have to make everyone *sure* that it was all the dog's fault?' I finished off this idea.

'I mean, it's not enough to just *say* something in court is it?' Plato went on, his words speeding up with excitement.

'No, don't you have to really *prove* it, so everyone believes you and not the other side?' I said.

Mum and Dad were turning first to me and then to Plato, as they followed the ideas bouncing back and forth. Except that for once we weren't taking opposite sides like we always had until now. I would have said it was like one hand rubbing the other, except I didn't want to risk annoying my brother any more – but it *was* just like that saying! The idea is that each of our two hands naturally helps the other one, and so one friend naturally helps another too – or even one sister and brother! I guess we had been a bit like someone whose hands are always fighting each other, which would make life tricky!

'Well, kids, I'll say this,' said Dad after another pause. 'Animals can have a trial too, that's in the laws Solon gave the city, yes. But, of course, *someone* has to speak for them,' he added softly. '*Someone* would have to speak for Tigris here, wouldn't they?'

'*I* will!' I said.

'*I* will!' said my brother at the same instant.

Mum's eyes turned quickly to look where Tigris in the corner was lapping his own bowl of milk. Suddenly my appetite returned. I smelled the sweet smell of bread in the air, and took a chunk from the bowl on the table. It was as if for the first time since I heard that howling down below, I was coming back to life.

There was still lots more to do.

'Dad, does that mean there has to be a trial in the courts? I mean, a real one?' I asked.

'Well, no, I think that, what with waiting to hear about war and peace, and arguing about them, the older citizens will be too busy to hold a trial for Tigris in court,' Dad answered, after he had also taken a mouthful of the bread.

'Then can't there be a sort of trial *here*, before anyone gets to take Tigris away from us?' squeaked my little brother quickly, and I definitely didn't feel like arguing against him!

'A trial *here*? Ah, but who would be in charge and who would do the judging?' our Dad replied almost as quickly. '*I* couldn't be in charge or do the judging of it, since Demos was complaining against me as well.'

'There must be *someone* he would have to allow!' I found I was getting braver now, because there wasn't much time left to find a plan for saving Tigris.

'Hmm, I have a meeting with other citizens early tomorrow morning, so I could find somebody there, yes. I could do that, if they would agree,' came the reply. 'I think we would only need one person to be both the President and our council of citizens to judge this case, I mean, if they were right for the job. But it would need to be somebody *special*,

46

someone who knew about running trials and judging cases properly.' He seemed to be talking more quietly to himself now as he stared into the distance.

So he agreed to try and find one for us! Tomorrow he would ask one of the important citizens at the meeting to return with him and take the double job of presiding over and judging the trial of Tigris. When Demos returned with his wooden collar to take him away, the dog would at least get a fair chance of going free.

'In a big city trial the citizens take charge and judge who would be chosen by drawing lots,' Dad went on. 'But I'm sure I can find someone who knows how to be fair, so that should be good enough for us at home. The man I'm thinking of was the President of the Council that judged one of the biggest trials the city has ever had – a trial of some of our top generals! Only one of the wisest citizens can be picked for President in such a case, so he shouldn't be too worried by our problem!'

It was still going to be up to me and my brother to save Tigris. The trial would probably make Demos twice as cruel if at the end he got his hands on the poor dog. Tomorrow was a *real* test of how well we could argue! A life depended on it, as well as the happiness of our whole household.

We both went and gave Tigris a pat before we left for bed. He was already asleep in his corner. He had no idea about tomorrow. He was better off than we were!

We decided we'd both be up early. We didn't have much time to work out how to save Tigris.

# Six

I had a strange night. Every few minutes, it seemed to me, I awoke with a shock as if it was morning. The world was still dark and cold, so I closed my eyes again. I often have dreams, but not like the ones I was having now as I slipped in and out of sleep! In one of them a Spartan army led by Demos marched through Athens right to our house. Giant men in armour broke down our door and came in with great shining swords and shields. They pushed me aside and grabbed Tigris, then they marched off again. I could hear our dog howling in the distance as they went away with him down the road.

In another dream, I was sitting in the courtyard on my favourite bench. My hands held a tangled ball of wool. I knew that I had to sort out *all* the threads or the city was going to be burned to the ground. There was already a smell of smoke in the air. I tried and tried, but I couldn't tidy the threads. I felt my hands sweating.

When I woke up, there *was* a smell of burning! It was a relief to realise this was only the kitchen slaves lighting the bread oven for the day's baking. Then one of the wise women who pop into my head said that the best smell in the world is the smoke of home, and I felt a sudden rush of comfort right through me, right down to my toes, especially after the fear in the dream.

There was a little light peeping through the window shutters. I decided to get ready and go down to wait for my brother. No sound came from his room next door yet.

The courtyard was still cold, but with a feeling of morning in the air. As I sat on my bench, the tree in the corner appeared out of the last of the darkness. The leaves turned from grey to green in front of my eyes, and the first birds began to sing. I pulled my thick wrap tighter around my shoulders and then there was a little *tip-tap* sound and Tigris came trotting over to nuzzle against me, before settling at my feet.

The peacocks were strutting around by the pond. I looked at them and at Tigris, they were so rare and he was just ordinary, as far as the world was concerned. I wondered how we were going to show that Demos *wasn't* telling the truth. How were we going to make that '*if* he was bitten' into a scorpion with *eight* creepy legs?

I started to go over in my mind what Dad had said about the laws the evening before. He had also told us that the laws Solon, my ancestor, gave to our city do not allow anyone to be seized and carried to prison without a trial. Only tyrants would do such a thing. But then, I thought, our bully of a big brother was planning to treat Tigris exactly like a tyrant would. He was going to take him away without showing that the dog was guilty of any crime. He had even threatened to bring a crowd and carry our pet off. Yet all he had done was yell and shout, he had not *shown* that his story was true. We just had to stay calm and work out how to prove that he was lying.

There was the thumping sound of Plato coming down the stairs. Next minute, he had rushed out into the courtyard and was walking up and down in front of my bench.

'Good morning, my sister,' he said, and he's never normally so polite!

'Good morning, my brother,' I replied, smiling. 'Are you ready to make the owl fly?'

'All right, I'm too sleepy to solve that! You tell me what you're on about . . . Proverb girl!' he said, this time with a cheerful grin.

'Well, wise old folk said that when the owl flies, that's the sign of good fortune – so we have to make sure it's ready to stretch its wings!' I answered – and now we were both laughing, not like usual when we're winding each other up!

Then we both sighed. It would be hard for us to argue against any grown-up. But Demos was famous for his speeches. He could take a crowd and stir them into a rage. As they listened to him shout and roar, peaceful men of Athens would turn into furious mobs. He had the trick of getting people to believe him. Even the best speakers in the city arguing against him found it hard to stop crowds being swayed by his angry words.

'You know, Potone,' said my brother. 'Demos *easily* could bring a gang with him if he wanted to. I'm sure he could get them to break into our house and take the dog away!'

The picture rose up again before my eyes, as if it was already happening. I could see the face of our older brother, almost purple with fury. He was bellowing: 'Seize that hound! Seize him! Put this collar upon him and drag him away!'

As I watched, his followers pushed their way through the door and into the courtyard. Their marching feet stamped over the ground. Cries of anger filled the air.

'Revenge for Demos! Revenge for Demos!'

They were almost upon us. I shivered with fear. And that was a good thing, because the shivering woke me out of that nightmare I was falling back into. In the real courtyard, birdsong was the only sound. Yet perhaps something like that was going to happen. Demos had such power in him!

Plato got up and began pacing around in front of me, faster and faster, like he always did when he was trying to think of an idea.

'Our teacher told us about this man who came to Athens a few years ago. What was his name?' He stopped and looked down at his feet for help. 'I know, he was called Gorgias, and he was from the island of Sicily. Anyway, he said he could teach even really dumb grown-ups how to win *any* argument. I wish he was here now with us!'

'Do you know his secret? What did he teach

people?' I asked eagerly, pushing away my longing about school for now.

He marched up and down some more. 'Well, he said if you wanted to win every argument, you had to make it seem like you knew *everything* there was to know.'

'How do you do that, especially if you *don't* really know everything?' I wondered.

'Mmmm,' said my brother. 'Yes, my teacher said the main thing was to use the biggest words possible, and repeat everything over and over, until it's sort of chased all the other ideas away from people's minds.'

'Well, go on, you show me how you'd do that for Tigris.' I was half teasing, but I was also interested as I said this. 'Make a great speech like that!'

'Umm, OK,' my brother agreed, a bit nervously. 'My fellow citizens, er, I am small and Demos is immense, I am young and Demos is mature, I am still learning many things and Demos seems to possess huge knowledge, but, er, but . . .'

And here he paused, so I decided to join in.

'But sometimes the smaller is greater than the larger, and the younger is wiser than the older . . .'

'Oh yes, nice one,' said Plato, squaring his

shoulders stiffly as he spoke. 'And the person who sounds as if he is wise may really know less than the one who is still learning . . .'

'Sometimes the little bird is wiser than the eagle . . .' I chimed in as he stopped to think.

'And the tiny ant may have seeds in its winter store when the wolf goes hungry . . .' my brother went on, looking pleased with himself.

'And the small dog may have more of the truth on his side than the big man!' I finished off.

We stopped and wondered together.

'That *sounded* pretty good, didn't it?' my brother asked. He didn't seem very sure.

'Yes, I bet that old Gorgias would have liked it!' I answered. 'But would it really help us win the argument? I mean, is whoever Dad brings to be our President and jury going to take any notice of that sort of clever-clever speech?'

'How do you mean?' Plato asked, stopping in his tracks.

'Well, what would Demos say if we went on like that?' I wondered aloud. 'Go on, you be Demos, what would you say?'

'Me? But . . . oh all right!' And my brother stood up as tall as he could and started to try and yell in his squeaky voice. ' "Is *this* a school room? Are we all going to sit and listen to these rotten kids while they show us how clever they can be? It's time to get back to the adult world. Let them have a good mark for their pretty words, but surely you can't take them seriously against *me*? They are just trying to win your . . ." er, what's it called, "your . . ." '

'Sympathy?' I suggested.

'Yes, your *sympathy*, that's it . . . "but don't fall for their cute little tricks. In the end, one word of a real man is worth a hundred times more than all the speeches of these, um, worthless brats." Isn't that what he always says we are?'

'I guess so,' I agreed.

Plato was really getting into the role of being Demos! He loves pretending to talk like other people!

' "Don't listen to their pathetic kids' stuff! Listen to me, I was *there*, I know what happened, and I'm worth a hundred times more than they are anyway. How can you for a moment trust the, er, the . . ." '

'Squeaky voice of a mere child . . .' I added.

For a moment my brother looked a bit annoyed, until he got back into the game: 'All right, yes good . . . "the squeaky voice of a mere child, when you can hear instead the strong and true word of a great man like me! One day I shall lead you all to victory against the Spartan enemy, and yet they dare to question my word! Here is your choice . . . " '

' "The twittering of children or the word of a true man." ' I rounded it off. ' "I tell you I was attacked by this vicious brute . . ." '

And here we both looked down at our Tigris, sitting peacefully under my bench with his tail flopping from side to side.

'No, you're right,' my brother said, and I was still a bit shocked to hear such words from him. 'You're right, Potone, even if you are being a bit of a sensible sandals, there's no point in us trying to impress the grown-ups with big speeches. Demos is always going to win if we do that.'

The proper morning was arriving now. Time was running out and we still didn't know what to do.

'We mustn't give in – it's the year not the field that grows the corn.' I was trying to cheer my brother up now by playing my old game of having a saying for everything! 'That means, the harvest only comes at the right time of year, however good the fields are. We'll get there – we just have to wait for the corn to grow!'

'As long as there *is* a harvest at the end!' He smiled back. 'What *else* could we try?'

'Well, the other day I wrote a story about how the hero Odysseus came home from his journey. You know about him from school, I suppose?' I asked.

'Yes, of course I've been told the story.' He nodded.

'Well, when he comes back in disguise, his dog Argus is the first to know who it is, and I wrote about it as if Argus was telling the story – so maybe we should try and tell Tigris's own story of what happened?'

'You mean we try and say exactly what Tigris would say?' he asked, a bit doubtfully.

'Well, come on then, let's have a try!' I prodded him.

'Er, right!' Plato said, clearing his throat. 'Umm . . . "Woof . . . I was just sniffing around the courtyard, trying to stay out of the way of those scary peacocks. I was feeling sleepy, and ready for a nap. I had curled up under one of the benches, when there was a big noise . . . and this man came shouting and yelling into the courtyard. I knew him at once. I've been frightened of him for a long time, ever since I can remember. Every time he comes here, he makes the fur on my back stand up in fear! And this evening he was even angrier than usual . . ."'

He stopped there, and we both looked down again at Tigris.

'What do you think?' I asked.

'Well, it was *nice*, I'm sure that man from Sicily would have liked it and my school teacher would too. But . . .'

'Yes,' I agreed, even before he had finished. 'It's *too* nice! Everyone would clap and smile, and sort of shrug. They wouldn't take us seriously, would they? And afterwards Demos could just say, "Well, you know, it's only two clueless kids telling a story about their pet dog, nothing to do with anything real," and he could yell his own story so loud that everyone would believe him when he said that poor Tigris was attacking the birds and then bit him.'

'Mmm,' said my brother. 'So that's two ways we *can't* win, isn't it? We can't make a grand speech, because Demos has made lots of them, and he's bound to do it better. And we can't tell Tigris's story like that, because it'll just make us sound, well, like we're two clueless kids . . . so what *can* we do?'

That was when I woke up the eight feet of a real

scorpion that would bite Demos. But at first it didn't seem very dangerous!

'Well, let me ask you a question,' I said. 'Do you think Demos *is* telling the truth?'

'No, of course not,' my brother replied, immediately. 'He's lying.'

'How do you *know* he's lying?'

'Well firstly because he's *always* lying, isn't he? I mean, that's the way he is. He's lying all the time! That's why he shouts so loud!'

'And then,' I added, 'because *anyone* who really looks at Tigris can see he couldn't have done any of the things Demos says. So that's two reasons to believe us and not him.'

'You'd think those two reasons would be enough for us to win the trial, if we could get dumb old grown-ups to see them!' said Plato, halfway between being excited and sounding worried.

'We must find a way to talk that gets grown-ups to listen.' I began to work it out more quickly now. 'The trouble with those speeches is that I don't think they would *really* listen to what we're saying, because we're only kids. But we know we're right! So, what do you do if you know you're right and a big loud bully is lying and you're still not sure other grown-ups are going to believe you and not him? How do you get to be believed?'

'It's two things, isn't it, when you think about it,' said my brother, carrying us forward. 'You have to show that he's lying and you have to say what the truth is. How do we *show* Demos is lying about Tigris?'

'You be Demos then, and I'll see if I can *show* you're lying.' I picked the idea up.

'Why do I always have to be Demos!' he complained, but then he smiled and started to shout. ' "I tell you this, er, this . . . whatdyacallit . . . this *hound* bit me with his savage fangs!" '

'With his *savage* fangs?' I said quietly.

' "Yes! That's what I said!" ' roared Plato, as fiercely as he could squeak the words. ' "His great brutal teeth sank right into me!" '

'Would you look down at this dog, please, and tell me what you see?' I replied, in my most harmless-sounding way.

'Ah, I get it . . . I *get* it . . . yes,' said my brother, stepping out of the game. '*I* do see! If we can ask him the right *questions*, he'll just show everyone he's lying! That's such a great idea, Potone, even if you are a bit proverby and sensible! I mean,

I wouldn't have believed you could think of it, but . . . you have!'

'Oh *thanks*!' I grinned back. 'Yes, what we have to do is to get *him* to make the chains for tying himself up by the way he answers our questions – then the grown-ups really only have to listen to *him*, not to us!'

'And I guess we also have to try and *show* them the truth, as simply as we can . . . *look* at this dog, do you think he could have done such a thing?' added my brother.

'One more saying? That's all for now, I promise!' I joked back.

'Oh, all right, then,' he agreed, laughing.

'The eyes are more honest than the ears! There you are, it's one of the best I know – but why is it true? Tell me that!' I said.

'Ummm . . . well, the eyes are what you see with – but what's wrong with ears?'

'The ears are always listening to what other people say,' I explained. 'So, I agree – we need to help people to *see* things for themselves if we can, not tell them in words!'

All our arguing today was on the same side. It was as if two streams that had been flowing in opposite directions were suddenly flowing together as one much stronger river!

'It's a pity we can't ask the peacocks though!' I said, watching them peck up seeds from the ground. '*They* must know what really happened!'

'Well, we'll just have to get our court to look at *them* too!' Plato replied, with a brighter smile.

I began to hope we really *could* do it! We'd sort of played our way into working out how to save Tigris.

But what would happen when Demos was really there, in front of us? And when real grown-ups were listening and judging?

Like a dark cloud passing over a blue sky, I remembered the picture I had of Demos leading a crowd into our quiet courtyard. If he wanted to, couldn't he just sweep us aside?

Soon there was the uneven bumping sound of Dad coming down the stairs and out into the garden. He was wearing his warmest dark cloak to keep off the cold when he went to the early Assembly. Mum came out and sent my brother inside to get his things for school. He still had to go! He left, promising to be back for the trial before the Assembly finished and the men came home.

I listened to my brother arguing with his helper

who carried all his stuff to and from school for him. He was a gentle man who never argued back! He didn't seem to mind the fuss as he walked just behind his schoolboy.

Mum and I sat with Tigris in the courtyard for the morning. It was hard to do my usual work. My mind kept going over and over our ideas about the law and Tigris and Demos and the trial we were about to have. Mum could see how hard I was thinking.

'Remember, Potone, who you are and where you come from!' she said with a smile. 'You *will* know the best thing to say!'

She also told me how happy she was to see my brother and me working together instead of arguing against each other!

'It is so nice to hear you say "yes and" to each other, instead of "but no" all the time! And I am sure you must have had much better ideas together than either of you would have had on your own!'

I listened to the spray of the fountain tinkling as it fell into the pond, and the birds still chirping up above. All these sounds became a kind of music in the air, a little harmony. Yes, I thought, perhaps there could also be harmony between me and my brother Plato.

That was what my happier side hoped. My sadder side also popped up soon after and asked me if I *really* thought all that peace and harmony would be strong enough when Demos returned, yelling that he could now take Tigris away. Wasn't shouting and stick-waving stronger in the end, than even the best arguing? It was as if there were two spirits, each trying to win me over to their view.

It was quite a warm morning, but I found myself shivering as the sad spirit won me over. Fear passed through my mind like a frosty breath.

# Seven

My brother came rushing into the courtyard, home from school. I could see he was also nervous. We shared a bowl of big raisins without fighting over them for once! We were too busy planning what to say when we had to defend Tigris against Demos. A little while after that, Dad was also home. But he wasn't alone. He had a man with him, someone I had never seen before.

When I first saw this stranger, I admit I was surprised my Dad had brought him here. He didn't look like the kind of person somebody important would even talk to, never mind invite into his house. He had wrapped himself in a messy robe with big holes in it. The cloth which had once been white was now a sort of dirty grey. The top of his head was shiny and smooth, while long strands of straggly grey hair hung down over his shoulders. He didn't have shoes on his feet, and to be honest he was . . . smelly!

I stared harder at the stranger's face. His eyes stood out, as if something was pushing them forward. It was the look in those bulging eyes that first made me feel his odd power. They were dark and yet they shone with a strange glow. His mouth was slightly open, as if there were words waiting to come out. Suddenly I felt a kind of magic in this quiet man with his ragged clothes and his messy hair. I could see my brother was feeling the same. His gaze was fixed on those eyes with their magical gleam, not on the torn robe or the dirty feet.

I noticed Tigris went over to the new arrival. He started ruffling the dog's floppy ears without looking down.

'This is my friend,' Dad said in his steady voice. 'His name is Socrates, and he saved my life when we were both fighting at the battle of Delium. Without him, I would never have come home. He drove off the soldier whose sword gave me the wound in my leg, and if he hadn't come at that very instant, I would have been buried on the battlefield that day.'

He said these words as if they were quite ordinary, and his friend showed no sign of even hearing them.

I began to see why these two felt comfortable together. They both had this peculiar calm, like still water with green depths.

'I have told my friend about the trial we need to hold here when my older son arrives. He knows Tigris is accused of biting Demos and that he will be taken away in a wooden collar unless it is shown this would be unjust. As I said yesterday, Socrates has been President in charge of some of the most important cases we have ever had in our city. He is also, though he won't tell you this himself, the wisest person in all of Athens. If anyone knows a true argument from a false one, it is my friend here. He has taught many of his pupils how to tell the truth from lies, and facts from mistakes. Now he is happy to be both the President in charge of our court *and* the whole jury of citizens for judging this case of ours today.'

Plato and I both stared at Socrates, who was still stroking the dog's head. *This* was the person who was going to decide our Tigris's fate. He was very different from other men I had met, but I decided I was glad he was here. I trusted him to be able to tell what was right. It wasn't only how Dad talked about him. Even without that, he made me feel calmer inside, as if he was someone who made life better for people.

As I was cheering myself up, there came a loud yell from behind us, in the house. Another moment and Demos burst through the door and stormed into the courtyard. I saw he was carrying something wooden that was obviously heavy. *That* was the heavy collar the law said he would have the right to put on our Tigris if we couldn't stop it happening!

Tigris had already crept back under the bench when he saw Demos arrive. I noticed that Socrates was watching the dog out of the corner of his eye. He had spotted how scared our pet was too.

'Bring me that rotten cur now!' Demos yelled in his fearsome voice. 'Why are you keeping me waiting! Here, I have the wooden collar for him as the law says I must! His *last* collar!'

And this man who was also my older brother began to stride across the courtyard towards the bench where I was sitting with Tigris underneath. I felt his eyes cut right into me as he got nearer and nearer.

'Wait!' My dad's steady voice rang out and even Demos stopped, about a step away from grabbing hold of Tigris.

'What is it *now*?' he hissed. 'I'm going to have my rights as the law says!'

'Indeed, you will have everything the law allows,' said Dad carefully. 'But first we must find out exactly what the law *does* decide about this case. Before you take the dog away, there is going to be a proper hearing. We have someone who has been in charge of judging great cases and has also spent many years thinking about how to decide between the truth and errors, between facts and lies. He's going to give us the right judgement on this matter according to the exact law of our ancestors.'

Demos spun round and stared at the stranger in his ragged robe and bare feet. His mouth twisted up in an angry grin as he answered: 'Ah, one of your *beggar* friends! Yes, I am sure he must be wise indeed! A perfect President and judge!'

Socrates did not seem to have heard this. His face stayed calm and he stood still, as if he was listening to another voice talking, a voice that nobody else could hear.

'Both sides in the case of Tigris will be given, as they would be in a city trial,' Dad said. 'And I assure you Socrates will be the fairest person you could have to hear the case! Besides, I am sure *you* have

70

nothing to worry about. After all, you are a great speaker, are you not? Your speeches for war sway the crowds every day, so surely you will have no difficulty in defeating these two mere children who are going to speak for their dog.'

For a second, I felt Demos was going to rush over and try and seize Tigris. The idea was rising into his eyes. There was a movement on the other side of the courtyard. The two men who stopped him yesterday began to walk over towards us. A dark shadow of angry fear passed across Demos's face when he also saw them. He put the wooden collar down with a clunk at his side, where it lay by his feet. I told myself he wasn't going to make the same mistake twice – even a really stupid fisherman won't be stung twice by the same jellyfish! That made me think of this bully being stung by a fish too and *that* made me smile, which was just as well as otherwise I might have burst into tears with nerves!

'Well, let's get on with it, since as you say, I have a bigger speech to give later. I want to make sure this brute is not able to bite anyone else before I do that.' He was staring right at me as he said this. 'Oh yes, and since your men took away my stick yesterday, I thought you would all like to see the special one I have brought with me today.'

In the flurry, I hadn't noticed that next to the wooden collar he had been holding a long stick. Now he had put the collar down, he waved it at us. This time the wood didn't have a bronze tip, but the metal had been sharpened to a point, like a spike. It was a deadly weapon. One blow would be the end of Tigris, or anyone else it struck. Demos gave another little smile when he saw the terror showing on my face.

His voice was like ice, but there were flames in his eyes, as my enemy-brother spat: 'Say what you have to say, then!'

In the old stories Mum has always told me, lots of girls and women get captured or even killed, or do wrong things and end up in trouble. But there are also some other women in them who are strong and even scary. When he threw out those words at me, I thought of some of *those* women. There was Athena, who as well as being the goddess of our city, was also goddess of just wars, the ones that people have to fight to survive. Then Artemis was the goddess of hunting and wild animals, even lions and wolves.

Even more frightening was Nemesis, who was the goddess of revenge! Almost all men are afraid of *her*.

Some, like Demos, might think a girl couldn't defeat them – but I was going to prove them wrong. I hoped Athena, Artemis and even Nemesis would be there on my side.

# Eight

I felt we were now at a crossroads where two paths led us in very different directions. One led to the happy place where Tigris was free. The other led to his death at the hands of Demos.

Plato stood up from the bench. I was very proud of him as he lifted his hand up to show he was about to speak and held his head high, with his spiky brown hair on top. He was silent for a second and then he began by asking a question as we had planned.

'So . . . do you say this dog was attacking the peacocks when you came into the courtyard, and that was why you . . . you . . .'

'. . . hit him with your stick?' I finished off the question, since he was getting upset even trying to say it. Our scorpion had begun to stretch its eight legs!

Demos jumped as if that creature had scuttled towards him with its pincers clicking! For a moment, there was a doubt in his eyes, I was sure of it! Then, with his hands rounding into fists, he roared his answer.

'What do you mean, do I *say* . . . by what right do *you* ask? I tell you, this filthy beast was about to kill my birds . . . my father's birds, whose mere feathers are worth more than all of you put together!'

Here our court President, wanting everything to stay polite as it should be during a trial, made a mild request: 'Please do just answer the children's questions and we will get on much faster, thank you very much indeed,' and he nodded for us to carry on.

'Well, then, since he doesn't want to answer that question,' said Plato. 'We'd like you to see what Tigris can *show* you by himself . . .'

And he called Tigris over to him. Together they walked across the courtyard to where the peacocks stood by the pond, warming themselves in the sun. As my brother and the dog came near, one of the big birds suddenly spread its tail feathers out wide with a whoosh. The poor dog immediately turned around, ran back to the bench and hid under it!

I was pretty sure by the sound of him, Socrates

would know to trust his eyes, as the saying went! With that, I turned to Demos and asked him our next question: 'Is this *really* a dog who would attack peacocks?'

Socrates said with a smile, 'Sometimes an animal can *show* the truth far better than people tell it with all our words! What an interesting thing to see, yes, it makes me wonder what else animals could show us, if we only noticed! Please do ask your *next* question, young people, and I hope it is as interesting as the others!'

It was Plato's turn to ask again.

'You still say our little dog went wild and bit you when you were stopping him from attacking those big peacocks?'

Demos simply spat on the ground in reply.

I decided to carry on as if he had nodded politely.

'Now I have a really big question to ask you . . . are you sure that our dog *actually* bit you? Couldn't you be making some kind of mistake?'

I had expected my big brother to shout and yell. Instead there was a strange silence. The longer this silence lasted, the more alarming it was! When Demos did reply, he started off almost in a whisper: 'Am I sure . . . am I sure . . . ? Well, I'll tell you what

I *am* sure of . . .' and now Demos's rage grew and grew until he was screaming the words as if he was trying to stir up a mob in the marketplace. 'I *am* sure that when I get my hands on this hound in a few minutes' time, I will show you who I am and what happens to anyone who tries to oppose me! One day the same fate awaits all those who try to get in my way! First the dog who dared to wound me . . . and then you dirty people, and lastly all those in the city who dare disagree with me about the greatness of Athens!'

If any dog has ever foamed at the mouth more than Demos did as he made these bitter threats, I would be surprised! That question had bitten him as sharply as any scorpion!

Plato carried on with the questions. We could both see we were starting to win: 'You'd *really* say you were wounded?'

Demos glanced back at the man who was judging our case, caught his eye and then managed to give an answer, even if he had to force himself to.

'Yes! I *would* say I was wounded! Badly wounded, too!'

'Wounded like Dad here was hurt at Delium?' I posed the next question to him quickly.

I noticed with a sideways glance that Dad was actually smiling as I said this. Demos wasn't smiling!

'Bah! Nonsense . . . I had a far worse wound from this . . . this monster's jaws!'

'You know how Dad's wound left a scar that we could all *see*?' Plato asked in a matter-of-fact way, as if we had not all been really upset by it.

'I suppose so . . .' muttered Demos, after a sulky silence.

I jumped into the little pause: 'And so, since *your* wound was so much bigger, it must have left a huge great scar too! I guess it can't have healed up so quickly either, can it?'

'That's what I tell you!' spat our older brother, not in a very brotherly way!

'Please will you let the court see what this terrible wound looks like?' Plato finished off, unable to resist copying a bit of the way Demos speaks.

The reply was even angrier!

'No! I will *not*! Wretches!'

In his fury, he was losing the whole argument. That was the moment when I saw we were about to save Tigris!

I felt now we had to make *sure* the grown-ups got the point, so I added another question: 'But why will you not *show* anyone the truth? If you wish, we can all turn aside, apart from our court President. And he has seen wounds and death in battle, haven't you, sir?'

'I have indeed seen many such wounds,' Socrates said, gently.

'So you won't mind if Demos shows you his gaping fresh wound, will you, sir?'

'I will not mind at all, not even one tiny bit,' he replied.

'There, Demos, now you can feel free to show him the great scar, and none of the rest of us will look,' Plato said and he spread his arms out when he made this offer.

As we knew he would, Demos refused to show the wound left by the dog. That was because there wasn't one! How much clearer could it be that Tigris, by his trembling, had shown the plain truth, while all Demos's outbursts had been lies? It was the man who had gone wild, not the dog!

Instead of showing his wound, Demos bellowed with fury: 'I *won't* be ordered around by these intruders here in the house that will soon be my own! I will have you thrown onto the streets, where you belong, the minute I can!'

I refused to be silenced by this bully's threat and finished the case, still in simple questions, right until the last moment.

'Are you *sure* you won't show your awful wound? How can we know it is there at all if you won't reveal it even to the citizen who is to judge the truth? And now instead, let's look again at Tigris . . .'

This last idea took everyone else by surprise. I saw Socrates raise his eyebrows, the most he seemed to show of what he felt. My brother and I kneeled by the dog. We gently brushed Tigris's hair aside to show the marks the stick made yesterday. There were the long red lines. We stood up again and then my younger brother spoke for us: 'Now I ask . . . who are we supposed to believe? Our dog who shows us his wounds, or that man who will not? Who was the *real* attacker, our trembling dog or that big bully?'

He stopped there. To my surprise I found that I had stood up from the bench again and Socrates nodded to me.

I wanted to finish off our shared argument: 'Some people think animals can't tell us anything. After all, they don't have words. But our dog Tigris has just shown us his whole story, hasn't he? Trust your eyes, not the big words your ears have heard from that . . . from Demos. How could this little dog have attacked *anyone*, peacocks or people? The law is clear. Our . . . our *brother* Demos has, well, he has had trouble answering questions even from kids like us, hasn't he? And now Tigris himself has *proved* that he couldn't have bitten anyone, not even a bird. We're both sure this man has no right to take away our dog. That collar must stay empty! Please . . . let our Tigris go!'

I finished, amazed that I had been able to make such a speech. I had stopped even glancing at our one-man President and jury of citizens. Now I turned towards him. I was sure I saw a smiling light in his dark eyes and even a look of delight passing over his face. He said nothing, but I knew I had made him happy in some way I did not really understand.

My bully of a big brother was *not* so happy. In fact, I have never seen a human face so far from happiness! Every moment of the trial had added flames to the fire of rage inside him. I still think that was all *his* fault, really.

# Nine

Dad was looking down at the ground where he sat in his chair, as if he was too deep in thought for words. Socrates had stayed standing all the time. Now he turned to our grown-up brother and, as if he was adding a final touch, he asked: 'Do you have anything else to say before this court gives its judgement on the fate of Tigris?'

Demos had been willing to let our family hearing go ahead because he was so confident about his own power to persuade people, as he did in the Assembly and elsewhere. He had been sure he would win. I could tell he was not so sure what to do now!

After a pause, he stood up straight and tall as if he was on a stage and stared at my brother and me.

'Would you choose to believe a dog and some fatherless children or a *leading* citizen of Athens? There is no other place in this city, or in the wide world, where anyone would doubt *my* word and accept the nonsense spun by these noisy brats! And anyway, I don't believe for a moment that they thought of all that for themselves! I am sure they were given their ideas by *someone* else,' and here he stared at Dad. 'What children could have come up with such questions? Is it possible? No, of course not! I am the victim of a trap – and the true aim is to deprive me of my rights. First, they want to take away my rights in law as the victim of the savage and dangerous dog they have brought into this house. More than that, I am sure the plan is to take away my rights to inherit the house itself and all that is in it! But I will have *my* peacocks! I will have *my* bowl of gold! *You*,' he turned again to our dad, his own dad, '. . . you cannot take away my rights to this house. You will not keep me from it much longer either! Soon enough it will all be mine . . .'

Here the court President gave a little cough and said politely: 'Thank you for those remarks, Demos, I think I am now able to deliver the judgement of this court's jury. I must ask you to leave your interesting thoughts for another time.'

Even so, Demos could not stop until he had said these last words: 'In the future, when I am the great leader of all Athens, I will take this city to a glorious victory over Sparta! We will have a vast Athenian empire! And then I will remember this day, and I will have my revenge on all of *you*, robbers, cowards, fools!'

Here he began tapping the metal tip of his stick on the ground.

'If you do not give me this dog as is my right, I will keep the wooden collar to remind me of the wrong you have done me, until I can have my revenge!'

There was another moment of quiet, just the breeze in the early leaves and a few little strings of song from the birds in the trees. Dad rose slowly from his seat: 'Before our court gives judgement, I must answer that last charge. My son, Demos, I can't prevent your anger at me, any more than I can silence your demand for war against Sparta. I am sorry for both, but they are yours to choose. There is no threat to your right to this house or –' and here he even smiled – 'or to the peacocks that you want so much. It will *all* be yours; nobody has any other plans. The court will make up its own mind about what happened yesterday in this yard and what right you have to this dog. I have nothing to do with that verdict.

'I *will* answer one of those last things you said. You accuse me of putting words into the mouths of these children, Potone and Plato. They are indeed very dear to me, as you are yourself, even if you do not see it. But they have no need of *my* poor words, I can assure you! Though I told them about the laws, they had not the smallest need for my advice on what to say after that! What you have heard here is two children speaking for *themselves*, in their own words.

'Now it is time to decide this matter, and I must just warn you, my dears –' here he turned to my little brother and me – 'that Socrates here may still give his judgement against your dog, and then you must accept it. Do you agree?'

There was a moment when the whole courtyard seemed to jump in the air, as I heard this. I nodded, and so did Plato, sitting next to me. We held hands and waited.

# Ten

We watched the strange man who had run the trial and was now judging the case between us and our own older brother. The fate of Tigris would be decided by the words he was about to speak. He shuffled his bare feet on the patch of grass where he was standing, as if he was hearing himself think.

Then Socrates started to talk, slowly and carefully, as if he was *writing* the words with his voice on the air. He spoke now as if for a whole jury gathered together from among the citizens to decide a real law case. After all, this *was* a real law case to us!

'So, our court has been asked to decide between this gentleman,' here, he nodded to Demos, 'and these children, in the dispute over the dog who I notice is still sitting there with them. This gentleman demands the right to take the animal away in the wooden collar that we can all see. He says the dog was attacking the priceless peacocks. When he tried to save them, he himself was bitten. That means the law of Solon gives him the right to remove the dog and indeed to kill it to prevent further harm.

'Potone and her brother Plato have spoken for Tigris, or rather they have asked his questions for him. At the end, they also showed us how he is too scared of these birds and this man, to have attacked either of them. Instead they suggest the man attacked the dog in a rage. Here, then, we have two different stories. How should we judge between them? Which is the *true* story?'

He stopped and stared into space, from where the voice which spoke only to him was giving the answer.

'You know, sir,' he turned to Dad, 'as a good teacher, I try my best to help my pupils sort out the true and false parts of the mixed-up arguments they hear. All kinds of people come to learn this one simple art of finding truth in a world where it has many rivals, such as lies and errors. To spot the arguments of truth sounds simple and yet it is the hardest art in the world to learn. Nobody is ever so wise that he cannot be deceived by a clever lie or confused by a big mistake. The false can sound true and the true may even sound false. But often when we listen carefully, and *think* about what we have heard, truth shines out to us with a bright light like the sun.

'Today, though, at first, I was unsure. It seemed to me that both stories sounded possible. Why should the dog *not* have gone wild, attacked the peacocks and bitten the man who wanted to save them? Then again, perhaps in a fit of anger *he* was the attacker, and the dog –' here he pointed to Tigris, sitting peacefully under the bench at our feet – 'and the dog was doing no harm to anything. I have spent my life weighing up the things people argue over and the different stories they tell. But the more I think, the *harder* it becomes to be sure. What then shall I do to judge? Or should the court refuse to give a judgement?'

I couldn't believe it! Was he going to leave us back where we were? What would happen to Tigris if he did that? He carried on, with a little smile on his face, in his gentle words: 'But if I do that, what becomes of justice? Like a good citizen and a fair judge, I *must* try my hardest to decide between the stories and make the best possible judgement. No court or jury will ever be *perfectly* sure of all the facts, when people speak against one another, each claiming the truth. There will always be reasons on both sides. Yet that doesn't mean we just give up and say we can't decide *anything*, my friends, does it? So, let us do our best here.

'On the one hand, Demos was present in the courtyard that evening. He has spoken as one who saw what happened with his own eyes. Why then should we not believe this gentleman who was *there*?

'On the other hand, Potone and Plato have asked him such interesting questions and they have also spoken for Tigris, who was also present.

'Two things have helped me to make up my mind. First, I have watched this dog with my own eyes, and, thanks to these children, I have been *shown* the marks on his back as well, and I have *seen* the nature of the man who made them. And second, I think that truth always asks better questions, and it is Potone and her brother who have asked all the good questions today. Demos is a grown-up. They are children – and yet he has not been able to answer those questions. The court now finds that Tigris is innocent and must be left in peace at home. You, sir, will have to take that wooden collar and metal stick away with you, I am afraid, and I hope you will dispose of them both before they do any harm.'

As he stopped, Demos rose suddenly. His stick came up with a swish and I thought he was going to strike out at the judge. Socrates did not even step backwards or blink an eye. He stood calmly facing the attacker when that metal point flashed in the evening sunlight.

Plato and I both screamed. Dad rose as quickly as he could to his feet and tried to get between Demos and the man he was about to strike. Was *he* going to be hurt instead?

'You saved me at Delium, Socrates, my friend, and now I must do the same for you in my own home!' Dad cried. I was sure the stick was about to crack his head as he almost fell into its path. Was this trial going to end with murder instead of justice? Was everything about to be lost after all?

The tightening of his arm told me that Demos, after hesitating, was about to bring his weapon whistling down. Dad stood firmly in front of the man who had once saved his life in battle. He was about to give up that life in return, protecting the guest from his own son!

My brother and I had both stood up, but we were frozen to the spot. Tigris stayed under our bench. Now with a bark, at the last second, the dog leaped out from his hiding place and jumped right up at Demos! Since Tigris was always so scared of him, our grown-up brother wasn't expecting that! He fell backwards onto the ground and his stick flew into the air and came down with a clunk of brass.

Demos groaned and tried to get back to his feet. The stick was only an arm's reach away. But Tigris stood growling at him in between, as he lay there on the grass. Everyone could see that even then the dog didn't try and bite Demos, just watched and waited! Still there wasn't any doubt that Tigris would have done *anything* to stop my big brother getting this terrible weapon back. Like Dad, he too would have given his life in the fight!

Tigris *had* saved the day. He had made time and, in another moment, the two men who were watching for trouble were standing over Demos. They had their hands clenched in fists and there was no mistaking what they would do if he tried to get his deadly stick back.

For an instant, the trial had almost turned into a fight and the court nearly became a battlefield. After it was over, and the stick lay on the ground, Dad and his friend stood hugging one another. They were both usually as calm as anyone could be, but now I could see them trembling. I guessed they must have hugged like that too after Socrates saved Dad from the Spartan at Delium!

After that hug, the court President and its whole jury, Socrates, walked over and picked up the stick. He held it in his hands.

Demos's last chance was over. Tigris was safe, and so were *we*, at least for a while! One of my wise voices said in my ear that now I was out of range of all the enemy arrows! At least, until next time there was danger.

Our big brother staggered to his feet. His eyes were wild but he knew there was nothing he could do here. He turned away from us all and walked towards the house. Over his shoulder came his final words for that day: 'Soon enough I will have this cur of yours! Meanwhile I must go and speak against your cowardly peace treaty, my father!'

He might win in the end. Yet on this day, the river *had* turned round and flowed backwards – and two kids had won against this wild man, who usually persuaded everyone he was right! Maybe Athena, goddess of our city, and Artemis, goddess of wild creatures, and even Nemesis, goddess of revenge, had helped me too!

#  Eleven

**T**igris trotted over to the man who had judged his case and set him free.

'You were lucky, my friend, to have these children to speak for you!' Socrates said with a smile, as he started to ruffle Tigris's orange-brown fur again. He turned to us: 'Many young fellows who are sure they are the smartest of people in Athens have come to learn wisdom with me. I don't think *they* could have done as well as the pair of you did today. The truth is also like Tigris here, isn't it? It needs people to speak *for* it, to tell *its* story. Without you and your questions, the truth could not have shown itself, any more than your dog could have spoken for himself.'

Mum came out and walked across the courtyard while he was talking. She looked peaceful now, calmer than I had seen her for a long time.

'You see,' she said to my brother and me, 'how much you can do if, instead of arguing with each other, you work together!'

'Ah,' Plato began – he wasn't going to accept this, even now! 'But how would we have learned to argue with that bully if we hadn't first argued with each other? We'd never have done it if we'd always just agreed with each other all the time!'

Mum decided it would be wiser not to answer. She would only have started another argument!

'Young man,' said Socrates to my brother, with a smile in his gentle voice. 'You must come and argue with *me* when you are older. Then we can learn from each other and see if we can find a little more wisdom together.'

I knew that Plato had been getting his ideas ready to argue with Mum. He stopped when he heard this. I really thought I saw light start to shine in his eyes. Suddenly in my mind, I saw him when he was older, still with wide shoulders and spiky dark hair, and rumpled robes, walking backwards and forwards as he tried to catch his new ideas in words for Socrates. I guessed that he had the same picture in his mind.

*I* wasn't there in that picture. Socrates had said

how well we had *both* spoken, but he only asked my brother to be his pupil. He smiled kindly at me, even now, yet he wasn't going to ask me to join him in searching for wisdom. Even *his* school, the wisest school in the city, had no space in it for girls and women. Amid the happiness of saving Tigris, I felt sad, as a harp sometimes plays a sad tune behind a happy one.

The wisest man in the city would not let me learn with him.

'But, sir,' I found myself saying softly. 'Won't you miss out on half the wisdom in the world if you only talk with half the people? Without *us*, your search will be only half a search! Half the questions that could have been asked will never be heard. Half the ideas that could be thought will never be thought.'

I didn't need to say who 'us' meant. He knew immediately. I saw my mum's eyes fixed on Socrates as he stood thinking about how to answer me.

His gentle smile had sadness in it. After a long pause, he answered: 'There is no such thing as half-wise, my dear, and so I think humanity will not be wise at all until everyone is part of the search for wisdom. In a future city, in a *better* city, girls will go to school, and some girls who are just like you will join the search for wisdom too. I am sure in that city women will make as many of the laws as men. Women will run the city at least as much as men will. But that will be when you and I and others have helped everyone realise that there are no good reasons for the way things are now. When people understand that, they will all want to live in a just city.'

Here he turned and smiled at the house men who had stopped Demos from attacking us yesterday and today.

'In that good city, my friends, *everyone* will be free to learn and no one's life will belong to another person,' he said, with a feeling for which my only word to write now is 'love'. There is no other word for that voice. The day which began with fear and hate was ending with hope and love.

Still I knew I would never be Socrates' pupil and search for wisdom with my brother. At that moment, I remembered lots of the gloomier sayings that I had kept in my store. I suppose people must have said them when *they* felt something was hopeless. The one that fitted how I felt best was 'you're only writing in water'. Since writing is my favourite thing that was the saddest idea I had ever heard.

I felt then as if a girl like me who wanted to learn and read and think was writing on water, doing something impossible. But I wasn't going to give up – even the fact that I knew this saying proved I had already learned plenty of things!

The breeze sighed in the leaves, and to me the song of the birds sounded a little sad. Perhaps that was their evening tune.

Socrates had said he was sure a better city would come. That was when I decided to write this story down. Perhaps by doing this, I am bringing that good city a step closer.

I was sure Mum would let me write it down on our mornings together. There's a lot more to do, but my wise women tell me that when a thing is well begun, then it's already half-done – so perhaps that's true of stories too.

# PART 2

# TRUTH
# AND THE
# PLAY

# Twelve

As I would expect, only a short time after our moment of success, my troubles were back with a vengeance! Maybe Athena and Nemesis had changed sides after helping us win the trial and they were against me now. They say the gods are like that. Or perhaps it was just my usual kind of bad luck, due to being born on the wrong day. We *had* saved Tigris, but it soon turned out that we had also stirred up a big nest of hornets by defeating Demos.

I had just *so* many sayings in my head in the difficult days that followed! Apart from the warning about not bothering hornets, the one that came into my mind most often was 'There's always another battle, even after Marathon'. Marathon *was* a great victory for the army of Athens over a much larger Persian army – but it didn't stop the war between

101

us. Oh no! As the saying goes, there was simply another battle and then another. Our one victory over Demos in the trial was like Marathon . . . it led straight to more battles, not to peace.

I had known bad times would return, but all my worrying didn't come anywhere near preparing me for what happened! It all burst on me suddenly – and it's *typical* that this was exactly when I was feeling better, a few days after the trial. The morning was sunny, the air was gentle and breezy, the leaves on the tree in the courtyard were brighter green and you couldn't help feeling hopeful with spring all around you.

It wasn't only me. Many people were full of hope. Just the afternoon before, Dad came home from a meeting of the Assembly and told us that he thought peace was now much more likely. A while ago, our General Nicias had sent a plan for a truce to the Spartan King Agis. Messengers had arrived saying that he was considering this proposal, and, along with many of the other Spartan leaders, he was also keen to reach an agreement. It's true, they hadn't definitely said yes, and there was even that extra threat of an attack on our own city if the fighting did begin again. But Dad said it was always like this and people became more menacing just before they actually made peace.

Then my friend Niko came round, which was another nice part of the hopeful feeling. Our mums have been best friends since they were our age, and we've known each other practically since we were born. Her mum went inside and upstairs to visit mine in the women's sitting room and we sat down together in our courtyard.

Niko and I have always been able to talk to each other about everything. She's quite small with green eyes and wavy brown hair that won't lie neatly like it should, and she's got this really big laugh, much bigger than you'd expect. It's one of my favourite sounds. Sadly, in the last year, I hadn't heard this laugh much.

That's because a year ago, her older brother, Pamphilus, was killed in another battle against the Spartans. It was the biggest shock and brought war much closer again, just when Dad was getting better from his wound.

In my first memories of him, Niko's brother was a bit older than Plato is now, tall and thin, with the same wavy brown hair as hers. He had these amazing green eyes too, and though he didn't have her laugh, he had this funny cackling chuckle that was another of the sounds I'd grown up hearing. For a big brother, he was fun too, always happy to run races, and help us make houses out of stuff lying around the courtyards at both our homes. The last time I saw Pamphilus, he knew he was going off to fight, but he was still giggling and mucking around like when he was a kid.

The message with the news that he had died had come a few weeks later.

Since then Niko had lost the laugh that fizzed into the sky. A lot of the time when we were together, she only sat and stared, as if her spirit was somewhere else. I tried to keep her company as best I could. There wasn't anything I could say to make her feel better. Telling people to cheer up when they have lost someone they love is another way of trying to catch the wind with a net. All you *can* do is be there and wait. I know that from myself, even though I was very young when my first dad died.

After so many years of war, our city has a lot of people with a silence inside them, where there used to be laughter.

Today, after sitting next to me on the bench for a while, Niko did start talking. But her voice was different from the old one. There was no music between the words, like there used to be. As she went on, she got louder and louder, but with none of the rising and falling that made her speech sing.

'They say your dad and that General Nicias and some of their friends are trying to do a peace deal with the Spartan monsters, so I've heard,' she began in that eerily empty voice, with a drumbeat of anger behind it. Every few words she paused and you could almost hear the fury banging inside her head. 'People are wondering how they can do such a thing! How can they even think about it when we've lost good men, like, like . . . my brother? Some people are saying we should throw these cowards out of our city, send them off into exile – why don't they go and live in Sparta if they like the Spartans so much? I don't know . . .'

You might think she was shouting and yelling. In fact, she said these furious things without any change in her voice, almost without any feeling at all, as if she was just reading out a message – except for those angry drumbeats I was sure I could hear in the pauses. I wanted to argue back, of course, to say that it was *because* he remembered boys like Pamphilus that my dad wanted to stop the war.

Talking wouldn't help. If our friendship was a tune, then any words I said now would be false notes. 'Don't ruin the music,' said one of my wise women to me, and so ... I simply waited for what would come next.

I could tell Niko had something more to say, and I wasn't really looking forward to hearing it. She paused here, and I heard the breeze and the sounds of water and the wuffling of Tigris in another corner. Then she seemed to lift more words from a deep pit inside her, where they were buried, waiting to be spoken. These words were so heavy that she had to struggle to raise them to her mouth, until out they came, one by one into the air.

'There's something else everyone's saying too, something I've heard when Mum has been talking to her friends. I'm not sure whether I should tell *you* though, Potone, you might not want to know,' and she stopped, as if she herself couldn't bear what she was about to tell me. She started again, looking away from me now, up towards the window of the room where our mums were talking. Then she turned her face and gazed into the clouds. 'Well, everyone knows your dad has changed how he sees this war. I mean, he went to fight the Spartans himself, didn't he? He wasn't a coward then, was he? So what people are wondering is, what's made a man like that grovel to our enemies after they have killed so many of our boys? They say your dad was once a friend of Pericles himself and *he* was the greatest fighter Athens has ever had. But now . . . now he's become a crawler, creeping on his belly to beg for peace . . . well, I mean, that's what *they* say, that's all I'm telling you . . .'

She stopped again. I could hear my heart thumping, like another drum inside *me*. Now I had to try and say something back.

'But Dad made peace before, with Persia, and nobody said he was a coward for doing it then. Everyone was glad when *that* war stopped. It's not true he has changed . . . wanting peace doesn't mean you're scared or, what was it, cowardly . . .'

I don't think she really heard me. She was hauling the next words up into her mouth.

'No, he *used* to be brave – Persia wanted to stop the other war, not us. He just agreed to let them give in, and in this war too he's been a brave fighter until now . . .'

'I don't think that's how it was . . .' I began – it made no difference; she was on her way again.

'Well, that's what everyone I hear says. My mum's friends think it's your mum who has changed him, and they say everyone in the city knows it too. It's all Perictione, that's what *they* say, she's turned him into a coward. It's *her* doing, really – I mean, I'm only telling you what people think . . .'

She carried on staring into space, as she waited for the next words to reach her mouth. Then they came tumbling out.

'The thing is, they're saying something else too . . . I mean, we all know your dad has been one of the really top men in Athens for ages and ages. He's talked to all the kings and leaders in other countries, and he's used to speaking to the Assembly and to generals and everything. So why would *he* listen to a woman when she begs him to crawl to make peace with the Spartans?'

She stopped and I tried again. 'It's true that my mum wants to end the killing, but so does my dad, it's what they *both* want! If she's made him try a bit harder, that's only by saying what she thinks and him listening, by them talking together . . .'

'No, but they're saying he wouldn't have wanted to give in like this, and no one in the city, well, no one among my mum's friends or my dad's either, believes she's changed him simply by talking. They're *sure* she must have used some kind of love potion, that's what they're all saying. And it's not just them who are saying it either – *that's* what I want to warn you about, Potone, it's for your own good I need to tell you this. Everyone is saying your mum must have put a potion in your dad's wine, so that afterwards he agrees with whatever she tells him . . . *that's* how he's become a coward now, so desperate for peace, when he was fighting the evil enemy himself before . . . at least everyone says that when they come to our house, and Dad and Mum too, when I hear them talking together.'

'But it's just silly, they can't really all be saying such rubbish!' I couldn't help replying, even though I wanted to stop myself. It was panic inside me needing to get out.

'Well, it kind of makes sense,' she answered, still without much feeling in her voice. 'My dad says there was a woman a couple of years ago, she was called Theoris, and *she* made these secret magic potions to change how people felt so that they lost all their own dearest wishes and deepest beliefs and all followed hers.'

'I haven't heard of her . . . what happened?' I asked, though I was terrified of finding out.

'Well, Theoris was taken to the main law court in the city, and there were lots of speeches against her, even the top citizens spoke, like that man Demosthenes who often wins the big cases, and the court found her guilty. She carried on lying and saying she had done nothing, but everyone knew she must have, otherwise why would the whole city have been talking about it? People don't just make up stuff like that! If everyone says it, then there has to be something in it, doesn't there?'

'Why can't a woman just have better arguments?' I kept trying, but it felt like net-waving now. 'Maybe that was all Theoris did too!'

'People aren't fools, they know what's going on.' Niko sounded almost satisfied now. 'And *they* say your mum has done the same thing as Theoris and not only to your dad . . . well, they say that your mum must have put the same potion in General Nicias's wine too, when he came to visit this house, because they know he's a friend of your dad, so that he would also grovel for peace like she wants . . .'

Niko said she was bringing the news to warn me . . . but it didn't feel like a friendly warning at all. I couldn't tell if she believed it too. I knew she was grieving and I guess she wanted revenge for her brother's loss.

'There's writing on some of the walls in the city too,' she ploughed forward. 'It must appear during the nights because there's always more in the mornings – and it says, "Perictione is a witch", "Stop the witch" and things like that – every day there's more.'

When she said *that* I suddenly knew exactly what was going on. I was sure, even if she didn't use the name herself.

'*Demos*!' I shouted. 'That's my brother, Demos! It has to be him! He's the one who's spreading these lies, I know it's him!'

'It's simply what people think,' she insisted. 'It's true, mind you, that your big brother *has* been telling the Assembly about it and other meetings also, that's what my dad came back and said, but lots of people think it's true anyway . . .'

'No! It's not like that, Niko! Can't you *see*? Demos is *starting* these lies . . . Oh, he wants to get rid of my mum and . . . and of me and my brother too . . . he's always been like that! I'm certain he's become even more furious since, well, I told you about it, since we had that trial of our dog Tigris and Socrates agreed with Plato and me, and Demos lost the argument . . .'

'Well, Demos says he can see what's going on in this house better than anyone, and what he's saying about your mum using these potions just adds up – well, it does for lots of people, because otherwise your dad has turned into this crazy scaredy cat out of nowhere, hasn't he? And Demos says she must have used drugs all the time, because otherwise why would a man like Pyrilampes have married her in the first place?'

Niko faltered here and I saw the bitterness of her grief. I half wanted to hug her, and half to shout at her.

'Oh! For goodness' sake! I can't believe . . .' I gave up arguing. 'Well, what happened to this Theoris when she was found guilty of making these potions?' I found myself asking, but I definitely didn't want to know the answer.

'That's *why* I'm warning you, Potone. They put her to death . . . and her family too. You need to try and do something, before it's too late! Get your mum to stop so your dad becomes his old brave self again! They say Demos is planning to bring charges against

your mum to the magistrates as soon as he can –
then they'll take *her* to court! You have to get her to
stop doing it!'

Inside me, I knew that this couldn't *really* be
something everyone in the city believed. The lies
were being stirred up by Demos, and Niko was
making it sound bigger and bigger, because, well,
because her mum and dad did half-believe it. Also, I
think, because she was feeling so angry and sad it
somehow made her feel better to have something to
be angry about. Still, even *some* people half-believing
this weird tale was about the worst thing, as if all
my worries had been rolled up into one ball inside
my tummy.

Before I could think how to reply, Niko's mum
came out into the courtyard, with my mum following.
I could tell they had been talking about the same
things. There was the same drumbeat of anger in
the air around them. They weren't chatting like
they usually would have been.

Then my mum said something to Niko's that
surprised me: 'Well, Dioni, are *you* also going to the
play tomorrow?'

It was like cracking an icy silence. But they had
been friends so long that whatever they had been

saying, Niko's mum still answered almost in their old way: 'Yes, of course, we wouldn't be left out!'

'Even though it's a play called *Peace* and it's by that writer, you know, Aristophanes, who's bound to say peace is a good thing, isn't he? Are you sure you're going to go?'

It was halfway between teasing and arguing as my mum said this. I watched the two of them, best friends who had become enemies for a while upstairs.

'We will be there, my dear, don't you worry . . .' the answer came.

'So, will you sit with us then?' my mum asked. 'Or . . . or are you going to avoid me . . . the great witch?'

I thought Dioni was going to storm out of the house without replying. A flash of fear and anger and all kinds of feelings together shone in her green eyes. She answered from some other part of herself, the part that was still a friend.

'Ah, I told you, that's just what *they* are saying, it's not me . . . we'll keep a space for you, dear, since you're always late, aren't you? Especially as this time, we'll be taking the kids!'

And they even managed to smile at each other.

As a family, we *were* always late. Niko and I also looked at each other as we heard this plan for going to the play being made. It was like a sort of dream. A few moments before, Niko was talking about potions and lies and plots and court cases, and now we were close together again.

That's because we've both *always* wanted to go and see a play. They're one of the most famous things about our city of Athens. Every spring, there's a great festival of drama, in the huge theatre on the hill up by the Acropolis, under the great new temple of Athena they have been building. Most of the plays are gloomy stories called tragedies, but there are also some funny comedies. I knew *that's* what this writer, Aristophanes, was famous for. He was always winning prizes for making people laugh.

The theatre was so big they said almost the whole city could go together to see a play. The men sat in the lower rows of seats, with the poshest marble ones at the front for the most important citizens. Then there were rows for women further back, and sometimes, like tomorrow by the sounds of it, even the children could go and sit with them too. That's where Mum and her friend were planning for us to meet.

115

For a moment Niko and I swapped smiles. They came back, out of nowhere, as if all the stress had gone away. Of course, we *were* still all stressed really – it just showed how much we both wanted to go to the play!

You know, like with our mums, when you have been best friends for such a long time, even if you quarrel or worse, old feelings must be in there somewhere, and sometimes they do come back, like everything is really OK. It would have been *so* nice if it had been! Even with all the horrible stories she had told me floating in my head, I was desperate to sit with Niko and watch a play for the first time, as we had always promised each other we would do one day. Things you have been wanting for ages can happen when you least expect!

Mum and Dioni nodded to each other – if not their usual hug, at least a sort of friendly sign – so Niko and I did the same.

'Tomorrow at the theatre then . . .' said my mum.

'We'll keep your places,' hers answered, and then they were gone.

# Thirteen

'**M**um,' I began, when we were alone together in the courtyard. 'Did Niko's mum . . .'

I stopped, it was hard to know how to say it.

'Yes, she did,' Mum answered, without me asking the question, which made talking easier. 'Did Niko tell you?'

'Yes, she did,' I echoed.

'Well, you mustn't take notice of all the nonsense people say,' Mum went on, firmly. '*You* know, and *I* know, and lots and lots of other people know, that your dad and I love each other without any potions. And anyway it needs no magic from me to make him want to find peace and stop even more people being killed. Of course we talk about it, and maybe I *have* wanted an agreement with the Spartans for longer, but we've each found our own way to believe in this treaty that General Nicias is trying to bring home.

And . . . and if she said the bit about me magicking *him* too, well, then you can see how crazy the people who believe such things have become.

'It's war, Potone, it's *hatred* and war that has put mad thoughts into people's heads. It's hard not to think strange things, dear, when people you love have died . . . And not only in the battles, but, well, you know, there's been another plague in the city too. Sometimes it seems like we must be near the end of the world! We have to *try* and make things better again, that's all we can do. I'm afraid, meanwhile, some people will fall for anything, with such strange goings on all around us.'

'It's my big brother who started the lies, though, isn't it?' I needed an answer to this question too. 'The rumours are all Demos's stories, aren't they?'

'Well, yes, that's another part of what's happening, I'm sure. Nobody is at their best right now, Potone, but *some* people are at their worst . . . fear is making him do and say things that he wouldn't when he feels better . . .'

I was surprised when she said this about Demos.

'*Fear*? You mean my big brother is afraid? He doesn't look that way to me!'

'No, I can see he wouldn't look like that to you,

118

Potone, but I know how afraid he is – I can see it sometimes in his eyes.'

'What's *he* afraid of, Mum? It seems to me everyone's scared of *him*, not the other way around!'

'Ah yes, the scariest people are often the ones who are the most frightened. You know, my dear, they try and hide their fear by scaring everyone else . . . Yes, he's *really* scared inside, believe me . . . scared of being left out, and also scared of not being as important in the city as his dad, maybe scared of not being able to impress him. You know, I think that's it, more than anything . . .'

She was almost talking to herself now, as we sat together in the breezy sunshine.

'He's always wanted to show his dad, *your* dad, how he's just as good, even better, how he's going to be more successful and more powerful and richer . . . You know, your dad doesn't really care about all that anyway, he's worried about other things, he knows being important is just, well, just bubbles on the surface of the river. But people can sometimes do really terrible things, my love, when they want so badly to impress a person they love . . .'

I sat and thought about this other Demos who had suddenly popped up before my eyes. I gazed across the courtyard to where he had attacked Tigris and where we had held the great trial and Plato and I had stopped him taking our dog away. Could that really be true? I wasn't sure – everything would look so different!

'But if he's so desperate to impress, Mum, he'll have really *hated* losing the argument, and that man, that Socrates who Dad likes so much, saying we had won against him!'

'Oh, I'm sure! It's the worst nightmare for Demos, my dear, I'm afraid so. He's even angrier and doing the craziest things, but inside I think he's sad really, because he feels he's failed in front of his dad . . .'

'So, you think that's why he's spreading these stories . . .'

'Yes, something like that . . . He's still trying to make up for losing and impress your dad with his power, even if it means . . . if it means calling me a witch . . . But those kinds of stories come and go, like the breeze, Potone, and truth is like our tree, here all the time, growing new leaves every year.'

This did fit with lots of things, but it was so much the opposite of how it had all looked till now! I needed more time to think, and meanwhile . . . there was the play!

'Tomorrow ... tomorrow, *are* we going to the play with you?' I said, after a pause, changing to a nicer subject.

'Of course, dear, you and Plato will both be there, and we'll sit with our friends,' she added firmly. 'And you'll get to see a really funny comedy – and you know, best of all, the main actor will be *Apollodorus* himself!'

Even in the middle of everything that was happening, I felt a bubble of excitement. Apollodorus was the most famous funny actor in Athens, probably in all of Greece, and even the wide world! Just by walking around on stage, he could make a whole theatre flood with laughter – and he was also famous for the way he argued with the audience, adding his own jokes to the play as he went along.

'Apollodorus!' I gasped, and suddenly the future, well at least the next day, looked much brighter!

Just then Plato came out into the courtyard. Mum told him about the play and how he was coming with us to see it. I could see the excitement on his face. Yet he just couldn't let anything be so simple!

'Our teacher has been going on and on about the plays, and the festival, he says how important it all is. But . . . but I think it's silly, making up stories and pretending to be in them . . .'

'How can you *say* that?' I began. 'Plays are the best! It's the lies people make up and think are real which are silly, not plays which everyone watching really knows are made up. No one thinks they're real, except a little bit while they're going on . . .'

This was getting quite tangled already! Before we both got started, Mum jumped in: '*Anyway*, we're all going, Dad will be down at the front, and you'll be with me and our friends, so you might as well look forward to it!'

Even Plato was happy really, he just wouldn't admit it! He had more fun arguing than agreeing, that's what I think . . .

# Fourteen

**N**ext morning, I woke in a whirl of ideas and feelings. There was everything Niko had said, which I could still hear as if she were talking to me now, in my room. Remembering her words made me feel sure something terrible was happening to us. On the other side was the idea of the play, which made the day look like it was lit up by extra-special sunshine.

Meanwhile, next door I could hear Plato starting *his* day – and it made me wonder if we were *ever* going to get to the great theatre at all. I doubted it, if we had to wait for him to get ready! Poor Doris, our nurse, only wanted him to put on his sandals! It wasn't simply that he wouldn't wear them. Anyone might prefer to feel the grass with their feet in the courtyard. But most people would say 'No, thanks' or maybe 'Do I have to?' or even just 'No!'. My brother said a lot more than that!

'Put on your sandals, dear, and then you can go outside and sit on a bench,' Doris began, briskly.

And this was the answer she got, in his squeaky voice, talking really fast as if he was discovering something new every second: 'I'll have to ask my feet about it. Do you want to wear a sandal, oh, left foot? "No, I don't!" Do you want to wear a sandal, oh, right foot? "Not me!" You see, nurse, it's not my fault, it's my feet. They don't want to wear sandals this morning. I wouldn't mind, but my feet really don't want to and it wouldn't be right to ignore what my feet think.'

'Don't be silly, Plato! I never heard of anything so daft. Who asks their feet what they want? Whatever next! Now, come and put your sandals on. Your mother will want you down for breakfast.'

As I listened to my brother arguing back again, I thought I could hear something else too, even though what he said was so silly. I heard his voice when he was older, a grown-up voice but still a bit squeaky, bouncing along full of the excitement of new ideas. It wouldn't be me who got to argue back then. Perhaps Socrates could do it, or the other pupils with him. I still knew that *I* was the one with whom my brother Plato had really learned to argue. Long before his famous teacher, he would have learned to argue by talking with *me*.

At that moment I was sure he would become famous for his arguing one day. Perhaps even more famous than Socrates himself. A long time ahead, people would still be thinking about his ideas – and trying to work out what was *wrong* with them, like I did as I lay there listening to him going on about his feet!

Another time I'd have liked to argue with him, and show he was all mixed-up about this too. I'd have told him that he's already inside his feet, so he knows what they want before he asks anything, because they're just *him*. And then I knew he would say *I* was wrong because every bit of his foot, his toes and his toenails too, had its own ideas and things about what it wanted! We could have gone on all day, all week, all year, even our whole lifetime! But not today! Today I just wanted Plato to get *ready* so we could go to the theatre and find our places and see the whole play properly.

I put on my best tunic with the glowing red dye. Down in the courtyard, I found Mum wearing *her* best gown with the purple pattern of little circles on the neck and at the front. She had her brown hair coiled above her head, rather than hanging down like on ordinary days. She was even wearing her golden brooch, but she was looking as if she was halfway through a long morning already, trying to get all three of us there on time! Dad must have gone ages before.

The biggest of the peacocks was opening out his feathers and giving them a stretch. Tigris had been sitting in a corner of the courtyard, out of the way of the birds. Now he wanted to come and say hello to me, so he trotted quickly over while the peacock was busy.

Out came my brother with our nurse. They walked into the courtyard. I watched him waving his arms and pointing up into the sky, as if truth was up there for everyone to see, as long as they just followed where *he* was pointing. He wasn't going to let go of whatever idea he was now on about . . . even if it meant missing the start of the play, the first one we had ever got to see!

'Come on, Plato, hurry up!' Mum nudged him, but she knew it probably wouldn't do much to help.

'I'm not sure I want to go, Mum,' he answered. 'I don't really think plays are a good idea . . .'

I knew perfectly well he was just trying to start us arguing again, and that he was looking forward to it as much as I was! I tried to resist replying, until something popped out anyway: 'You're the one who's pretending, even more than the actors! You *know* you're desperate to go to the play!'

I could see him perking up when he saw the chance of a good argument before breakfast. Then he must have decided to keep it for another time, and went off to get ready – just as well, because otherwise we might still be there, arguing with each other, long after *Peace* had finished.

We were almost ready at last and the carriage driver came to say that the horses would be round soon. My brother was still wanting to go back for something else, even as we went out with Mum into the roadway in front of our house, leading down to the city. Behind us, we could hear the whining of poor little Tigris, who was feeling very left out!

By then, the carriage was already there, with the pair of horses at the front, shuffling and stamping their hooves and the metal of the two big wheels shining from being specially cleaned.

The carriage driver helped us onto the wooden bench facing away from the horses, then climbed onto the front seat, and we started on our journey. Now my brother was happier – he was excited to be rolling along like that, as the horses began to trot faster. The wheels scraped and screeched on the loose stones in the roadway while we rumbled by.

There was still a bit of trouble, when Plato tried to take off the heavy cloak that had been wrapped around his shoulders over his tunic. Mum said he had to keep this cloak on, it was winter, even if the sun was already shining. He said if he felt hot, then he *was* hot and it didn't matter what anyone else said he *should* be feeling. Luckily, before another full-scale argument could start, we had turned to go up the bigger road towards the temple and the theatre.

There were lots of other carriages and also a crowd of people walking to the festival. As we crunched over the bumpy ground, snatches of things people were saying to each other floated to my ears: 'But I hear the Corinthians are trying to stop Sparta from agreeing to the treaty, that's what the latest messengers say . . .'

'They say the Spartan army is already on the march towards us!'

'The Oracle has warned of danger! The gods are said to have refused the last offering!'

'I was told the Spartan king is about to sign the treaty – isn't that good news!'

'No, let's keep on fighting, not beg for peace!'

The nearer we got to the theatre, the more people flowed together and the louder this hubbub of chatter became. Even though I was *so* excited to be nearly at the Festival of Dionysus, the god who specially loved our drama, I felt a sharp nip of worry after hearing these stray voices. What if the Spartans really didn't want to agree to peace? Or what if our own Assembly of citizens didn't agree to it, even if the Spartans signed? And then as we came to the theatre itself, I overheard something much more worrying:

'Look! There's *that* woman, what's she called . . . Perictione . . .'

'No? You mean the one who makes the love potions . . . ?'

'That's *her*! They say she's used them to make her husband desperate for peace with Sparta like her!'

I knew it was only a few words reaching my ears by chance, almost nothing, stray straws of gossip

129

blowing in the wind. I looked at mum, her face was frozen with worry for a moment, then she gave me a reassuring smile.

We reached the great theatre, then for a while it was just too incredible to think about anything else! Excitement was bubbling around me – I wouldn't have believed so many people could fit into one place. Dad must already have been sitting at the front with the important men of the city. We got down from the carriage and went the other way, towards the back, climbing past rows of benches. We clambered higher and higher and up and up the side of the great bowl of the theatre, away from the stage, which was waiting, empty, for the magic of the actors to bring another world to life.

At first, all the benches we passed were full of men, shouting, laughing, arguing, eating and drinking. Finally, we came to the first rows of women, when we were much nearer to the top, by the rim of the bowl. Everyone here was wearing bright robes, embroidered with all the colours you could think of, green and blue with touches of red or purple. Dotted around were children like me and my brother, our high voices like the songs of birds among the shouts and calls of the grown-ups.

Here it was as if I were walking through a whole city of women and children. Then amid my happiness, this idea suddenly became a nightmare picture. I knew that when a city was conquered by an enemy, and there was no agreement to save anybody, all the men would be killed and *every* woman and child would be taken away and made into a slave, sold for money by the winning soldiers. This would go on and on until the whole city was so empty, it seemed it never had any people at all.

I went on past the rows of laughing and chatting women and children, here to enjoy our Athenian festival, but what I saw now was *us* being led away in tears by the Spartans, our fine robes turned into rags, with chains rattling as we went. And when I turned around to check, instead of the rows of yelling and joking men, I saw . . . for a moment, I was *sure* I saw mounds of bodies, heaped up everywhere I looked.

I knew that when the armies of Athens had defeated places which supported Sparta, they had done this to all the people who lived there. It was meant to make other cities surrender more quickly so they didn't meet such a terrible fate themselves. What if there was no treaty and the Spartans and their allies surrounded *our* city in the spring? What if we refused to give in? If they defeated our soldiers, wouldn't the same thing happen to us, the fate our men had brought to others?

This horror might be what people call a blind dream, one that doesn't tell you the future, strange ideas that come into your mind because of how you are feeling. But then again, it could be a real warning of things to come!

I imagined being a kitchen slave or a house girl, taken to a city far away. The last I would see of my brother Plato and my mother would be them being sold to other households. I would be among strangers, in a foreign land, where I could hardly understand the way they spoke Greek. Every day, I would awake cold on a stone floor, and start to sweep and carry and light fires in the dark, long before my ... my *owners* got up. And always, I would remember the bodies of the men of Athens, piled high like sacks of grain.

For one moment, the nightmare covered up the world around me, like bitter-smelling fog. The thing that cleared the air was the call of a voice: 'Hey, Potone! We're over here!'

Niko was more like her lively self as she called to me – and we squeezed excitedly along the row to the gaps she and her mum Dioni had kept for the three of us. Plato sat on the other side of Mum, then I was next to Niko, then came her mum, Dioni.

I felt jumpy from the day before, and I'm sure she did too. But today we were both so keen to enjoy the play together that we didn't want anything to stop us. Even so, I couldn't help saying something about yesterday.

'You know that story you told me ... I mean, about what people are saying ...'

'What about it?' she said, and the old Niko seemed to vanish again. I knew it was pain and loss speaking so bluntly, but it was hard not to get angry.

'Well, you're right some people *are* saying those things, I mean, that's what I heard as we came up here,' I went on, trying to prevent myself from arguing. 'And I can see you meant the best in letting me know, I'd have been really panicked if I'd heard them out of nowhere, so thank you ...'

'That's OK,' she nodded, with a little flicker of her smile.

'It's just that when we're here, looking out over *so* many people, all those women and men down to the stage ...' I waved my hands towards them as I said this, 'well, you can see how huge this city is,

133

and how most of them don't know anything about me or my mum or you or your mum, or any of us and I'm sure they don't care either. It's true my dad is probably a bit famous here, but I don't think that means this whole crowd is really bothered about little old us!'

For an instant, Niko even laughed – at the idea of this great sea of people being worried by us tiny fish! Then I felt I had to try and get hold of that moment.

'It's good to be warned, especially about Demos and what he might do, but the idea that all these people here are worried about my mum's supposed magic potions is a story without a head, that's what the old folks would have said. Or they might have said it was going along the wrong road. Or missing the target by the size of the whole sky . . .'

She stared out at the wide ocean of Athenians below us, and nodded. Then she smiled as more of my sayings came pouring out, one after another – that's always been a bit of a joke between us.

'You're probably right, Potone, and it's nice to hear your old proverbs, but even so . . . keep an ear open for what's being said, before Demos does something worse, like trying to bring charges in court as my dad said he might. I know my mum and dad are a bit, well, they're a bit sort of upset these days ... maybe I am too, it's hard ...'

Her eyes started to shine with tears while she was saying this – I nodded a little so she would know I understood. She carried on trying to put her feelings into words: '... It's hard when ... when you've lost ... I don't know ... you get all sorts of ideas in your head, and you don't really know what to do with them, ideas you wouldn't have had before ...'

I nodded, while the huge audience seemed to make one giant muttering sound around us.

'I do know inside, that your mum wouldn't ... wouldn't do *that*, whatever Demos, or Mum or Dad or anyone says ... and I don't want more boys to die, like ... like my brother, so if we can have peace, let's try ... It's just ... well, I find it hard to imagine us and the Spartans being anything other than enemies and I do think in the end we'll have to fight till someone wins ...'

'Yes, I can see that might be,' I said, touching her shoulder. 'And it must be horrible for you ... well, I was so little when my first dad died, but I can still feel it somewhere, all the time, and I understand how hard it would be to want peace with the people who have done *that* to you . . .'

It felt better to hug than try to put more thoughts into words. After that, we sat together and waited for the play to begin.

I was looking down more happily over the rows of people, eager for the few minutes to pass before the action on stage began. Then among all the laughter and the talk, there came a strange sound. At first, I thought it was men shouting excitedly to each other. But this was something different. The noise got louder and louder, cutting through the babble like a sword through piles and scraps of cloth. It wasn't singing exactly, yet the voices all joined together, so there was a kind of angry harmony.

For a moment, all I could hear was a roar without words – until *they* became clear too: 'Athens first! Athens first!'

The bubbling noise of the rest of the audience died down. Now the air was full of those words. The play might be called *Peace* but someone didn't want this to be a moment for peace at all! Someone wanted this to be a moment of war.

'*Athens* first! Athens *first*!'

In between the chants, there came the clash of hands clapping, like drums banging as an army marches in step to them. The chant stopped suddenly, and the ordinary chatter began to pick up, but the calm pause didn't last long. One voice on its own called out over all the happy sounds of the audience: 'Death to Nicias!'

That was the name of our general who was trying to get the Spartans to agree to the peace treaty – Niko had even said yesterday Mum might be using her potions on *him*! I really liked what he was doing, but not everyone agreed with him – I already knew who had to be starting this chant, who hated the treaty most of all! I followed the sound with my eyes, down through the rows and rows of men towards the distant seats near the front.

There Demos was, standing up and facing away from the empty stage, so that he looked over the flood of faces behind him. Today his white robe was edged with bright gold with shining threads of silver across the folds. Now he was chanting all on his own: 'Death to Nicias! Death to Nicias!'

His wasn't a lone voice for long! In another moment, a booming chorus was carrying his words over the whole theatre: '*Death* to Nicias! Death to *Nicias*!'

As if he had yelled into a vast cave, the call became a great echo, bouncing back to him from the darkness beyond.

'*Death* to Nicias! Death to *Nicias*!'

Just listening made all the worry about my big brother flood back – the old fear that he would take Tigris and kill him, and the new fear that he would make everyone believe my mum was a witch who had magicked my dad into wanting peace. I had pushed the threat away, but now here it was again!

The fierce cry sank down, but the quiet was like the gap between the crashes of thunder in a big storm. Demos soon began the chant to make the next roll of thunder: '*Peace* is shame! Peace is *shame*!'

He called the words out twice and then in a giant outburst, the audience took it up, men and women all over the theatre now, as the energy reached higher and higher, right to the back where we were sitting:

'*Peace* is shame! Peace is *shame*!'

All this time, my eyes were following the bright

metal on the stick Demos was waving with his right hand. Sunlight gleamed in flashes, like streaks of lightning to go with the thundering voices.

I looked round at Niko. That chant was so close to what *she* had said she felt only the day before. She started nodding in time to the shouts. Her mouth stayed tight shut but I could imagine those words echoing inside her.

Then I saw Niko's mouth silently copying the chant: '*Peace* is shame! Peace is *shame*!'

I'm not sure she really even understood what this meant. She was feeling a power that made her want to join together with most of the people in that huge theatre. As long as the chanting went on, they were buzzing with the same excitement. And Demos was where it started. If *anyone* was using magic to change how people felt, it was my big brother, not my mum!

'*Peace* is shame! Peace is *shame*!'

It was as if Demos had sent out this magic spell into the air, enchanting Niko and her mum too with all those other people. A furious crackle fizzed above us. I wouldn't have been surprised to see a fork of lightning in the blue sky.

That thundering chant stopped and there was

another pause. The strange charm of war lost its hold immediately, and all those people who had been stuck together by it came apart again and felt as separate as before.

I was hoping it was over, but then Demos called out his new slogan, and again his power spread from front to back across every part of that giant theatre. Rows and rows of people were pulled along by the same rhythm.

'*Cleon* lives! Cleon *lives*!'

I knew about Cleon. He had been the leader of all the people who wanted the war to get bigger and bigger, until the year before, when he died in a great battle that also killed the fiercest of the Spartan leaders. That's what had really given both sides their chance of making a treaty. No agreement would have been possible with Cleon around. His name still *meant* war, and this chant was a way of saying, 'Keep fighting! Never stop fighting!'

'*Cleon* lives! Cleon *lives*!'

The call seemed to come from deep inside the crowd now, from the whole group, rather than one person at a time. There weren't many who were left out, like me, the few of us for whom the charm didn't work!

'*Cleon* lives! Cleon *lives!*'

Repeating this seemed to send many people into a kind of waking dream. The echo inside my friend was so strong that she started to mutter 'Cleon lives!' under her breath, though I don't think she even realised.

I could understand from Niko, and also from my own life, why people who have lost those they love can't let go, and I saw how that would make stopping a war very hard. But I almost couldn't bear it, such a call to death! Then suddenly, to my relief, everything was still, with no more chatter or chanting.

There was a moment's eerie silence.

How could such a large crowd have become so quiet? I turned and looked over the top rows of benches. High above the theatre, I could see the white columns of the temple that had recently been finished. It was the most beautiful building ever! A line of statues stood along the front, above the columns and under the roof. They were painted all kinds of bright colours, and between them the marble shone with a pure blue, like a perfect sky. This new temple to Athena was standing watch over the theatre, and over the whole of our city.

The sight gave me strength and I tried to force what I had been hearing about war and even about my mum to the back of my mind. The play was about to start.

# Fifteen

All around the theatre, there was a rustling like the wind over a field of corn when the actors appeared, as if by magic. They got so quickly into place. They were a long way down below us, but I could see them clearly. They were dressed in many-coloured robes and their faces were hidden behind big wooden masks, with odd curly mouths and empty eyes and huge noses. Somewhere out of view, musicians suddenly started to play, with the thud of a drum and the high peeping of pipes. It sounded like a mad dance tune!

The first bit of the play was *really* strange. It was all about this crazy farmer, who was, of course, the star, Apollodorus. His harvests had been messed up by the war so he wanted to go and find Zeus, king of the gods, and beg him to bring peace back to Greece. Then, he said, all the farmers could get on with growing food for everybody, in between sitting under the trees and enjoying themselves too. The big problem was that since the gods all live high on Mount Olympus, he had to find a way of flying up to meet them. And that was where the story got weird!

I suppose in more normal stories, he might have flown on a giant bird, or just been carried by the wind like magic. Not in this play! Oh no, nothing was so simple! Here, he rode on one of his own farm animals, but it must have been a very peculiar farm, because the creature was a giant dung beetle. That probably sounds more mad than funny. The trouble with telling you about the play is that what made me laugh was how Apollodorus *acted* the story. Everything in *Peace* was perfect for him to *make* it funny.

In our theatre there's a big crane that lifts an actor up, so he can pretend to be flying. It's normally used in the gloomy tragedies for the gods to soar above the humans. Here instead, Apollodorus pretended he was wobbling on his giant beetle as the crane towed him to and fro over the stage. Obviously riding on a dung beetle *would* be pretty smelly, so he kept grabbing the huge wooden nose on his mask and making being sick noises as he went along.

While Apollodorus was wavering around high up (it's a *really* big crane!), he also sang little songs to go with what was happening in the story. They all sounded kind of familiar, but also different, and they were the thing everyone liked best of all! He clearly wanted us to join in. Everyone certainly *did* when he sang an old song for little kids that's meant to be about the wheels on the cart going round and round, except he gave it new words:

> '*The wings on the beetle go up and down,*
> *up and down, up and down,*
> *the wings on the beetle go up and down.*
> *Yuck! It stinks!*
> *The farmer on the beetle goes up and down,*
> *up and down, up and down,*
> *the farmer on the beetle goes up and down.*
> *Yuck! He stinks!*
> *The dung on the beetle goes up and down,*
> *up and down, up and down,*
> *the dung on the beetle goes up and down.*
> *Yuck! It stinks!*'

The whole theatre was bellowing along with this, especially the 'Yuck' bits, when I heard Demos trying to start another war chant: '*Traitors* out! Traitors *out*!'

I could see him standing up and facing over the ranks of men watching the stage. Were they going to join in with him again, now that the play had started? Which would be the more powerful: the spell that Demos cast with the chants or the rival magic from the stage and Apollodorus's songs? There was a longer pause than before, and then some men near the front did take up this new shout of war: '*Traitors* out! Traitors *out*!'

As if he was trying to reply, Apollodorus then started a new song about his dung beetle. It was another tune everyone knew from when they were young, but also not with quite the right words!

> '*Dung, dung, glorious dung,*
> *nothing quite like it for getting stuff done.*
> *So follow me, follow*
> *fast as Apollo—*
> *But please do not swallow*
> *this glorious dung!*'

Next, Apollodorus started some crazy stage business. He asked each side of the theatre in turn to give him a wind to help his beetle to fly faster. He turned to the north side and called out to them – and of course he got the rudest noises back! The same with the other three sides, one after the other! Now the silly songs and fart noises Apollodorus had stirred up and the great chants of war were crashing into one other across the theatre, with the play going on between them.

The whole audience was being pulled to and fro between peace and war.

Meanwhile, the flying farmer was nearing to the top of Mount Olympus, where the crane began to lower him down. He still had a few rude jokes of his own to spice up the action: 'If you don't like our play, then you know what you should do ... you should stick to the gloomy tragedies!'

He even seemed to be turning towards Demos as he said that! Then he added something sillier: 'How does the bell on this beetle go?'

We all roared back: 'We don't know!'

'Ding-dung, ding-dung, of course,' he answered snappily, as he wobbled down towards the floor. The whole stage was now the mountain, home of the gods, or so he thought. But when the hero started to look around, he saw no gods at all. Then one of them appeared, in a shiny mask, stalking up behind him.

We all yelled out: 'He's *behind* you!'

It turned out this was the god called Hermes. Sometimes he's a messenger, which is why he had wings on his ankles – like I remembered when I was rushing down the stairs to save Tigris. Now he was more like a caretaker. He had been left to look after the furniture on Mount Olympus, he said, while all the other gods went away.

When he heard this, Apollodorus staggered with shock and then as he clambered to his feet again, he asked *why* the gods had gone. How could they possibly have deserted Athens and all of Greece? They were fed up, answered Hermes, because the people only worshipped one of them, the god of war, and ignored all the others. Zeus wanted nothing more to do with these people who always worshipped war.

Apollodorus added some songs to the farmer's pleas to be told where to find the gods now. As he was pleading, he burst out with:

> 'O, caretaker Hermes,
> Don't be a tease.

*O, caretaker Hermes,*
*do tell us, please!'*

And he also gazed at the sky and cried out:

*'O, Zeus, Zeus!*
*Please send us your news!'*

At last Hermes gave in and told the hero that if he wanted to end the years of fighting, he would have to look for Peace *himself*, and not expect Zeus or anyone else to do it for him. The trouble was War had thrown her into a deep pit, and covered over the top, so it would be very hard to get her back.

Now Apollodorus set off to find this pit, once more riding on his beetle. The crane lifted him right up high again and he began singing his loudest song yet:

*'Ten dung beetles flying through the air,*
*ten dung beetles flying through the air.*
*And if one dung beetle should swiftly*
*        disappear . . .*
*There'd be nine dung beetles flying through*
*        the air!'*

The song went all the way down from ten to nine until he reached *no* dung beetles and each time one vanished, he lurched as if he was falling off. He still had time to wave and encourage the audience in singing along with him. The war chanting had gone quiet while the actors were talking about the gods having vanished. Being deserted by *them* was too scary an idea to yell over! But as the hero flew off after that scene, that storm of noise had also begun again. The song about the ten beetles boomed around the theatre, and on the way, it was met by the next war chant.

I could hear Demos was trying again to get this one going: '*We* will win! We will *win*!'

Some people did take up his words, making them crash in waves of sound onto the stage where the farmer was looking for peace – but the silly song about beetles was at least as loud for now.

Meanwhile, on stage Apollodorus came back down to earth and pointed to a spot on the ground which he said was the lid over the deep pit where Peace had been thrown. You could see it was a different colour to the stage floor. He picked up a great coil of rope and began to unwind it, tripping every so often as he did so. The rope was obviously meant for pulling Peace out of the hole.

He knew, of course, it was too hard to rescue her alone and so he held out his arms trying to get people from the audience to come and help – but nobody did. Instead onto the stage came another line of actors. I knew they were called the chorus, and they all spoke together. Every play has them – they make the sad ones sadder and the funny ones funnier by the things they say and do.

On they rushed, talking straight to the audience:

*'Don't ignore us,*
*we're the chorus!'*

Pretending no one was noticing them, they added as if they were desperate for attention:

*'We're the chorus,*
*you'll adore us!'*

Then standing in a row, this chorus got hold of the long rope, unwound it completely and began to pull. As they did this, they sang another silly song, which was even catchier:

*'Heave-ho and up she rises!*

*Heave-ho and up she rises!*

*Heave-ho and up she rises!*

*Peace will come this morning!'*

Apollodorus waved his arms to make the audience roar along, especially with that last bit – even so, nothing came out of the floor which was meant to be covering the pit. There was no sign of Peace anywhere.

Meanwhile Demos was calling loud and clear: '*Blood* and sweat! Blood and *sweat*!'

He was trying to bring back the *excitement* about fighting, and you could hear the chant rising and pushing against the funny song already swirling around the theatre.

The mood was against him, but Demos wanted to conjure up the fierce passion that we heard before: '*To* the death! To the *death*!'

The comedy now had a stronger hold on the theatre, and his chants faded into silence before they could really grow. They never even reached my friend Niko. Anyway, she was too busy like me singing '*Up she rises*' and waiting to see if Peace would be rescued at last. All that time, the chorus had refused to let go of the rope, though she seemed to be buried too deep for them to ever pull her out. Now they all started to sing a more rousing song about never giving up:

> We shall not, we shall not let go,
> like a tree with roots deep down inside the
>     ground,
> we shall not let go!

The whole audience was caught up in *this* tune. Everyone in Athens had heard something like it being sung by the supporters of different wrestlers at the big wrestling matches, which were as popular in the city as the plays. In our family, Plato loves watching the wrestling almost as much as he likes arguing. I glanced over at him and this was definitely his best moment! His eyes were shining. He was really ecstatic as he bellowed out the tune of one of his favourite songs. Even Niko on the other side of me sounded happy as she sang along.

Eventually, at last, pulling that rope *had* to work, with so much support! A trapdoor in the stage popped open and Peace was lifted up by another crane.

She flew into the air with a loud cry, half-laugh and half-shriek. It was the funniest thing to see, and yet it was also really exciting. All the actors holding the rope fell over too, adding to the rumpus!

They were getting late on in the story now and because this was a comedy, that meant they were getting towards the happy ending. The hero got back on his beetle and flew home. But he wasn't alone any more. Peace came with him and so did the chorus and everyone else on stage. They began to enjoy a huge great party together, celebrating a bumper new harvest. All this time, Apollodorus kept joking with the audience, stepping in and out of the play: 'What do you call a play that ends with a big harvest? . . . Corny!'

He brought back one of his earlier jokes which fitted now: 'Knock, knock!' he went.

'Who's there?' we roared.

'Peace!'

'Peace who?'

'Peace *off* if you can't stop fighting!'

Then the farmer and a woman called Plenty, a friend of Peace, who had been rescued from the same pit after her, got married to make the ending super-happy. Apollodorus turned to help the audience sing them a wedding song, but it was more than that, it was a song for *everyone*. It was made using another tune from the big wrestling matches. When the fans want to show they won't ever stop supporting their favourite wrestler, there's a great song they sing, half-rousing and almost sad at times. Apollodorus had changed the words a bit, but this was another tune that everyone knew and could join in. It started with just him on stage singing and then the chorus came in and slowly the noise rose, as he brought in different sides of the theatre like with the wind earlier.

Eventually this song became a great anthem, sweeping round the audience, from the men in the marble seats at the front to the women and children right at the back, like us:

> '*Walk on, walk* on,
> *with peace in your hearts,*
> *and you'll* ne-ver *walk in chains,*
> *you'll* ne-ver *walk in chains . . .*'

This was finally as loud as any of the great war cries, even the biggest ones that had gripped the audience before the start of the play. It also seemed to answer the terror *I* had felt when I saw the picture of all the women and children in our city taken away and sold as slaves, while the men lay dead in piles. In the song, peace was the cure for this fear – peace beginning in all people's hearts.

Yet after all, this same crowd who now sang about peace being in their hearts had been swept up over and over in war chants. Do we have both kinds of music inside us? Can everyone join in with both of them at one time or another? I wondered if there was even a more warlike side in *me* than I had let myself notice so far.

Still this song about walking with peace in our hearts became the winner today. At the end of the play, there was one great peace song roaring around the whole theatre. Apollodorus turned to Demos, who had been his rival, with a last jingle of triumph:

> '*You're not singing now, you're not singing now,*
> *You're not singing, you're not singing,*
> *You're not singing NOW!*'

That was another one from the wrestling too – something fans yelled at their rivals after *their* hero has lost!

Desperately, Demos tried to strike back. He wasn't going to give in easily to this other magic, the funny peaceful kind! I could see him far below me in his gold and silver robe, waving the stick with its shiny tip in the sun. As I watched, he pointed that stick towards someone in the front row of marble seats and called out: 'It's *your* doing! Cowards like *you* are bringing shame to our great city!'

And then one last time too, he chanted: 'Keep *Athens* great! Keep Athens *great*!'

I knew exactly who he must be pointing that stick at, even though I couldn't see from this far away. It had to be his own father, my dad, Pyrilampes, where he sat with the other leading citizens right by the stage.

I felt everything inside me sink with a *whoosh!* I couldn't move.

Then Demos added one more chant and that changed everything for me: '*Peace* is poison! Peace is *poison*!'

Of course, I knew what Demos was doing! He

meant to remind everyone of the stories he had spread about my mum using potions to make my dad and other men want peace!

I had had *enough*! It felt like *we* were really the target of the war chant here!

There he still was, as he had been from the very beginning when we arrived, in the far distance below me. It was a long way down from where I was sitting, there among the women and children, in our happiest clothes. I didn't really stop to think of a plan. I just *found* myself moving along the row, passing the few people between me and the steps we had tramped up on the way here. Nobody minded – I was too small and quick to stop them seeing what was happening on the stage. I thought I heard my mum calling after me, but I didn't turn round.

When I got to the stone stairway, I let my feet set off down, steadily, one step at a time. It made me think again about Plato and *his* feet that morning – was it really only that morning? With a shock, I saw now he had actually been right about something! My feet *had* decided for themselves to go down these steps, like he said feet could, and the rest of me just had to go with them.

I went on by rows where people were singing or

chanting in different ways. In places, the war cries were huge – especially the latest one, 'Peace is *poison*!'. But in others, they were still roaring out about not walking on *alone* or not letting *go*. It was like travelling from war to peace and back again, feeling the struggle spreading across the whole city as I went lower and lower.

Now I was passing the last of the women's rows. I heard one of my wise women telling me briskly that of course I must do something about Demos now, not go on living a hare's life! What she meant was that hares are animals who run away from everything. Well, that's OK if you're a hare, isn't it? But who wants to be a human and live like that? My feet clumped more firmly on the stone under them after that!

I felt stronger and stronger, though I wasn't sure exactly what I was going to do. I just knew I had to do *something*. Below, less distant now, Demos was still waving his stick towards Dad and I knew what he must be saying, even if his voice was lost in the criss-crossing of more and more shouts and tunes. He *had* to stop – that was the idea filling my mind. And *I* was the one who was going to stop him!

More pictures were coming into my head. As if it had been someone else, I saw myself running down the stairs at home and out into the courtyard trying to save Tigris. Then I was listening to myself with Plato trying to work out what to say in the trial. I saw the trial, with the stranger, Socrates, standing and listening so carefully to every word we said.

The next picture in my mind was Demos turning away after he had lost the case – and just for a minute I thought I noticed a sad expression on his face that I hadn't seen at the time, like Mum had told me. Then there I was, sitting with Niko in the courtyard. Now I saw us both from the other side by the tree. I gazed at the stunned look coming over my own face as I was listening to what she was saying.

It was as if I had gone back along the road I'd taken in life, in the other direction to the one I had come by, as I was going step by step down the huge theatre. On the stage, which was also much nearer now, the wedding of the farmer with Plenty was over and all the actors, including Apollodorus, were dancing. As they jumped around, they were grabbing handfuls of seeds from a big bag and hurling them into the rows of people sitting in front of them. One of the actors explained that these were barley seeds from the last harvest – to plant for an even better harvest next year.

Seeds whistled past my head as I went, like barley hail! People in the audience stopped their chanting and singing to try and catch them, as if they really *were* good luck for the year ahead. Maybe the barley was even meant to be a sign of peace and the better life it would bring – *if* the treaty was signed.

Mind you, none of those seeds got up as far as the rows of women and children at the back, so all the good fortune, if that's what it was, was being caught by the men. The actors called out for them to pass some back, but I don't think any seeds of the peaceful future ever got that far.

While these thoughts were passing through my mind, I had got much closer to Demos. He was near the stairway, towards the end of the second row. The flute and drums had started to play a dance for the actors to say goodbye; it was almost the end of that story. But it was crunch time in *mine*!

I was about to face the man who had been the scariest person in my life for as long as I could remember.

The men around were starting to notice me too, because normally there weren't any children or women down that far. I had gone into their territory.

What was *she* doing? Perhaps they thought I wanted to get as close as possible to see Apollodorus! And that *could* have been the reason too, if I hadn't had this much more important one.

Now I was coming to Demos himself. I knew he would be able to hear me talking from here. He had seen me and was watching carefully. He stopped everything else. It was time for me to speak! Then right at that second, a wave of my old terror came crashing over me. I had this sudden feeling that I was going to turn around and run all the way back where I had come from. I'm sure if I had done, *he* would have started to jeer at me as I went and we would have been the victim and the bully again, like we had been before the trial of Tigris started to change everything.

I clenched my hands so tight the nails began to scratch my palms. I expected him to start shouting at me now – but he didn't. In fact, I noticed he took a small step back, without lifting his eyes off me. I couldn't read his face – it was almost like one of the masks the actors were wearing on stage ... His brow was creased with lines and his mouth was like a sideways line. I couldn't tell, though, if he was gathering himself together to act after he got over the surprise of finding me here. Or was it something else? If I hadn't known him from before, I'd have said he was worried.

'So, peace is poison, is it, Demos?' I forced myself to begin.

'The *true* people of our great city know that . . . but *you* wouldn't understand, would you?' he began sneering back in his usual way. Yet he hesitated as he spoke and his voice wasn't quite as strong. He looked around, as if he was hoping help would come. I even wondered if he was about to call some of his supporters to push me away. Then I noticed that the men on either side of Demos had turned round and were looking at me and back at him. The one on his left was tall and tubby, with long fair hair and a bushy beard. The one on his right was small and thin, with sharp blue eyes and deep lines so he looked as if he was frowning all the time.

Now I had something else to worry about. What were *these* two going to do? I pressed my feet down harder onto the stone. I knew I mustn't give away the smallest sign of fear, whatever I felt inside. It was like entering a lion's den. Just one hint of weakness, and they will leap at you – if you don't back off, maybe they won't come for you.

Demos's sneer might not have been as strong as

usual but it still made me think of the growl of a crouching beast, waiting to spring. His hand tightened its grip on the stick. I couldn't take my eyes off his clenching fingers, even though I knew it would have been better to show no sign of fear.

I tried to push forwards with what I wanted to say. 'You think my dad, *your* dad, is being charmed by my mum's poisonous potions, do you?' I asked, and, as I said this, I did look Demos straight in the eye. 'You think she's *made* him into a coward and that's why he wants peace, is that right?'

Demos didn't like being asked questions – I knew that from our trial! There was a pause in which he couldn't reply, though there must have been lots of words rushing into his mouth. Instead, he took just another tiny step back – it was hardly a step at all, more of a little movement, and all the worry in me began turning into hope, like the sky changing colour just before the sun rises.

I could *see* the extra effort he was making, as he stood stiffly upright. He was trying to find his old voice, the one that made the big speeches. But it wouldn't flow. Only little snatches of the big tune were playing.

'I don't know any *other* reason . . . what else

could there be ... everybody knows there are potions ...'

In our trial, we had won by asking Demos questions that he couldn't really answer, or didn't want to. I felt I was winning again now. But there was a big difference! This wasn't like the trial in the family courtyard, with Socrates keeping everyone in order and help nearby. It felt as if here, *anything* could happen and the trouble was that the less Demos could answer the questions, the more his anger showed, first in his eyes, then on his face and finally in the way he was acting. His shoulders tightened, so that they rose up towards his ears. He moved forward a step. There was no Tigris by me either, to surprise him and knock his stick away! And no Plato to distract us all with another of his ideas! Dad was too far away to intervene.

Was Demos about to attack? Around the theatre the songs and chants bounced and boomed, but now the sound seemed far away from us, in our own struggle. This had to be *our* own moment of truth, with the actors still dancing and scattering the barley of peace. I was sure if I gave way now, I would never get another chance to put a stop to his bullying. Demos would tear our family apart, and carry on spreading his terrible rumours. Who knew where that would lead?

The story of Theoris hovered over me, like a nightmare.

I became certain that if I looked away, or even blinked, he *would* strike. We carried on staring straight at each other. I knew any minute he was going to make a move. I felt myself tensing, to try and dodge the blow when it came.

I was hardly aware of anything else, so it was a total shock when the man with the fair beard, next to Demos, suddenly shouted: 'Shame upon you, sir! How can you think of striking this child? Drop that stick at once! I've put up with your nonsense for the whole play, but now you go too far! This folly is the fruit of all your hatred and war fever!'

Demos turned suddenly towards *him*, and I wondered if he was going to attack this stranger instead of me. On his face now was pure rage, his eyes were wide with it, his mouth had opened as if to let out a war cry, though he was still too surprised to say anything. Then, before he could do anything, something even *worse* happened! The small man on his other side, with those blue eyes, made a quick movement and darted across in front of my brother,

166

with his hand pointing towards the big man who had spoken. At first, I thought he was pointing . . . then I realised he was holding a dagger!

'Traitor! Why should *she* be allowed to bring her snivelling for peace here, among men who want *war*, war to the death! *I've* put up with the rubbish of this play – it's just stuff on stage, but I warn you, sir, there are limits to the patience of true Athenians! Stay out of the way, keep your cowardly views to yourself!'

There was a clatter – in *his* shock at what was happening, Demos dropped his metal-tipped stick and it landed on the stone at his feet with a ringing noise. The small man leaped at the sudden sound, as if he thought he was being attacked. His knifepoint wavered in the sunlight. And then without warning . . . a great stream of barley seeds poured down from the stage on top of him, as the actors hurried to empty the sack before the play finished completely. Was that pure chance? Or had they seen something wrong?

'Yurgh!' cried the man with the knife, starting to lose his balance but still hanging on to his weapon. If I'd thought about it at all, I would never have done what I did next – but there wasn't time to think! The stick was lying between my brother and me – I picked it up among the heap of seeds on the ground, like hailstones from a storm. Before anyone else could move, to my own amazement, I just whacked the small man on the leg as hard as I could manage with the metal tip. It was all one movement, as if it was being done completely by somebody else!

I don't suppose I hit him *very* hard, but I was close to him and the stick was sharp and, more than anything else, it was so unexpected, especially when he had just been covered in barley seeds from above. He collapsed to the ground with a howl, letting go of the knife as he clutched his leg with both hands. I've never been in more danger, but at the same time it felt like the silliest bits of the play, when everyone was rushing around in circles, calling things like 'Help!' and 'Emergency!', tripping over ropes and each other.

Now, of course, more men noticed something was going on. As if we had become part of the drama they were watching, they began to call out:

'Hah! That'll teach you!' roared Bald-head from the front row. 'Keep your thieves' daggers at home in future – don't bring them to our festival!'

'Yay! Good shot, young lady!' Young and Ginger cheered from further along the row.

'Outrageous! Call someone at once!' Greybeard stuttered, waving his arms wildly.

While all this hubbub went on, Demos bent down and grabbed the knife himself. I was still holding the stick. The small man had staggered to his feet and was now hopping up and down among the barley moaning, and then the big man grabbed him by the arm.

'Ha! Great strong soldier *you* are!' he jeered, as he tightened his grip.

Demos and I stood looking at each other, me with the stick, and him with the dagger. It must have seemed as if we were about to have a weird duel. But we didn't fight. To the sound of the music from the dance, and the small man's groans, and with the songs and chants beyond that, we came to a standstill together, and then . . . I just burst out laughing. It seemed to me that the total craziness of the play had come off the stage, like the shower of barley seeds, pouring into our lives! I was also laughing from relief too. At first, Demos looked blank when he heard me laugh – then he joined in, and I realised I had never ever heard him laugh before. The sound was surprisingly tuneful, not at all like the yelling I usually heard when he was around.

I'd laughed more in the last couple of hours than I had for ages. It was as if the play had reminded me how good it can be to laugh with other people, and how you can even laugh at your worries. I was amazed at what I was able to just *do* while I was finding things funny. It looked as if the me who laughed was also someone who could fight back, if she really needed to! The only time that person had peeped out before was when I jumped on Demos and pulled him over to try and save our dog Tigris. Afterwards that seemed to me like the sort of thing I would never do again – but now I was not so sure! Maybe that really was part of me too and I just had never noticed before!

My laughter had left a big smile on my face as I looked at Demos standing there with the dagger. Then gently, I handed the stick to him and gave a little bow, like a soldier handing a weapon back to an enemy, as a sign that the battle between them was over. I meant it, but it was also a kind of joke between us – that's why it worked so well. He also smiled, bowed back and took the stick from me. Now he was standing there with a knife in one hand and the stick in the other. He might have looked fierce, but actually I could tell he felt silly. The fury had boiled away like steam into the air, leaving nothing behind.

I wonder how many funny things are really scary, except after a while they lose their scariness. The play had been like that with the gods leaving Greece and Peace being buried in a deep pit by War. The whole story *should* have been scary, but instead it came out funny while it was being acted.

There were still things that needed to be sorted out in *our* lives but now I felt I could do it.

'*You've* been spreading around all kinds of crazy tales, Demos, haven't you? I bet you're behind the writing on the walls that my friend Niko has told me about, saying my mum is a witch!'

Even this somehow sounded less ... well, less *serious* at this moment. It was still a scary idea, but I found myself talking as if I was telling him off for doing something daft, something he should be ashamed of rather than a huge, terrifying threat. He looked down at the stick and the knife, one in each hand, and kind of shrugged, almost like a child who has been caught out – and he gave an awkward little grin that I knew was a way of saying sorry.

'. . . I really thought that was what had happened, Potone. That's honestly what I thought . . .'

'Then it's *not* true what Niko says, that you're going to try and bring charges against Mum for . . . for using potions to make Dad want peace? You wouldn't really, would you?'

I would never have been able to *say* this to him before! He would have raged and threatened – now he shuffled his feet and spoke quietly, almost softly.

'No . . . no, I'm not going to do that . . . It was just . . . it was just . . .'

He waved the knife and the stick awkwardly, as if now he was trying to use them to say sorry. Those weapons had been so scary – yet here they were almost funny.

Meanwhile, the big fair-haired man was marching the small man away, still limping – I must be a bit stronger than I think, and perhaps a bit more warlike too, if I have to be. It seems I can hold my own if I really *have* to.

Now we could also have an ordinary chat about all the things that had been tearing us apart before.

'You know Dad's always wanted to make peace, look what he did with Persia . . .'

'Yes, but he also went to fight the Spartans . . .'

he argued back, more like my *younger* brother, without the old fury.

'True,' I said, I could even let myself agree with him a bit now. 'So, he wasn't a coward then . . .'

'Well, Potone, why is he plotting this awful peace treaty with Nicias now?' he asked.

'Because, Demos, he's a peacemaker,' I answered, ignoring the way he put it. 'But wanting peace doesn't mean you can't also fight when you have to, does it?'

We both couldn't help laughing as I said this, thinking of me thumping the man who had the knife, and him toppling to the floor among the barley seeds with a howl. The laughter from the play had driven the fear and anger away – at least for now.

'No, I agree, it seems some peace-loving folk can pack a punch too! I still think, you know, *this* time the treaty is a big mistake, even if it worked with Persia. That was long ago and the world was different . . .'

'Well, that's OK, isn't it?' I didn't need to argue about this. 'We won't all agree, but that doesn't make everyone who disagrees with you about the treaty a coward or a witch, does it? Lots of brave people want peace, without poison and charms being used on them!'

'True, yes,' he nodded, with another grin – he had a nice grin when he let it show. *'You're* pretty brave, Potone, aren't you? I mean you were braver than I was, when that man had the knife out, weren't you?'

'Well, I've also spent a lot of time being worried – *you* know that . . .' I was amazed, but I could even say this to him now.

'Umm, yes I . . .' he stumbled.

'No, you don't have to *keep* saying sorry . . . It's just, well, I can see now that there's more ways to be brave than I thought, and also more ways of being scared, you know . . . and some people are maybe afraid of anyone else seeing how scared they are . . .'

I left it there, even now, this was as far as I could go – but it was enough. That was how truth arrived in our family, in the theatre, on a wave of laughter.

Now Demos put down the dagger and the stick and, at last, it was only *him*.

Inside me, I was nodding to my mum – she really *had* been right about my big brother. I was so used to showing that everyone's ideas, especially my brother Plato's ideas, were *wrong* that it took me a moment to admit how true *her* idea about Demos really was. He was scared and sad, because he felt left out and he was so worried about not impressing everyone he wanted. Mind you, that didn't mean he wasn't scary too, especially from further off – the chants he had started were echoing higher up the rows of the audience, even at the end of the play.

I really *saw* what Mum had meant, how someone like Demos can be both scared and scary. Maybe the two things even go together.

'And I may be young, but I do know making peace isn't *always* wiser than fighting back,' I went on, getting towards the end of *our* drama. 'For all anyone sees now, *you* could be right about this treaty not being a good idea – but that doesn't mean Peace isn't better than War, only that true Peace is always hard to find. She's bound to be hard to get out of the pit where War has thrown her. I think the longer the war lasts, the deeper the pit gets too!'

The dancing came to a stop, the last seeds of barley scattering pit-a-pat among the watching rows of people. One final stray seed flew by Demos and he caught it, in the hand which had just put his stick down. Then, with a serious look, he took a step forward, and held out the barley towards me. I stretched out my right hand and he dropped it there. Apollodorus himself noticed, we were so close to the stage! He called down to us: 'Your own piece of Peace, my friends! May it grow into a good harvest for you!'

And that was how Peace came out of the play and into our family – whether she was coming to the whole city or not, she had come to *us*. It all happened in a weird rush, with daft things and scary things all mixed up – and I still don't really know where so much anger and fear had gone to.

Another strange thing was, like I had said, to stop our fight, we didn't even need to agree! Trying to persuade Demos about the treaty itself would have been like ploughing the stubble in a field that had already been harvested – it would have come too late, bringing nothing more. In my mind, the wise women were also smiling.

'Well, here comes our dad,' I said. 'This is *your* chance to write the last act of the play, isn't it?'

'Um, how do you mean?' he asked, exactly like my younger brother does when I use an old saying he doesn't know.

'It's your chance to sort things out properly,' I explained and he nodded and turned, holding out his hand to Dad as he came up. They looked each other in the eye, and each gave a little smile, but nothing needed to be said as they clasped hands. Then they hugged.

I felt the weight lift from my shoulders – right now, I didn't have to hold the family up by myself.

As I gazed around at all the people surging out of the theatre, laughing and joking and some still arguing too, I knew the future wasn't going to be easy. Even if there was peace in the family *and* between Athens and Sparta, it might be that neither would last. Niko's story, and what I had overheard on the way in, also showed that some people really did believe the lie, even if it seemed *obviously* rubbish to me, about my mum making potions, and who knew what trouble that could cause?

I mean, you can think different things about a peace treaty. Demos might be right and folk like us who wanted peace *now* could be wrong. You have to decide that sort of stuff for yourself. But there's no *way* my mum is a witch – yet there are folk out there, ordinary Athenians, who seem to think she is, or at least they are OK to repeat the story they've heard about her. Demos wasn't going to make more trouble about it, so it would all die down for now – but still those weird rumours would be out there in the future somewhere in the city, even if almost everyone forgot about them right now.

You just never knew when that rumour could catch fire again, one spark was all it would take to make a blaze. With a shock, I saw that what happened to poor Theoris could happen to almost any woman in this city. It could be my mum or even me or any of us. Athens is ruled by what people here can persuade each other to think – and that includes lies, mistakes and dreams as well as all the better ideas.

Someone needed to sort that problem out! Maybe Socrates was only at the beginning of doing that.

Lots of problems weren't solved and many would never be. But *our* family war was over for now, a gift from *Peace* and from Apollodorus and from the laughter which made the whole world feel different.

# Sixteen

A few days later, Dad came home from the Assembly with the news we had been waiting for. General Nicias and Agis the Spartan king had now agreed to sign the peace treaty. But he warned us the citizens of Athens could still refuse to accept it. Demos did speak against the agreement – he hadn't changed *that* much! After all, he still believed the treaty was wrong, and he still really did love impressing crowds. Nothing would ever alter that! But on that day, the longing to stop the war was too strong, and Nicias was asked to sign for Athens.

It *seemed* peace had come to Athens. Our city would certainly be safe from the Spartans for the spring. We would see the leaves on our trees once again. Relief flooded over me – even though I knew it might not last.

I felt then that I am really *lucky* in some ways.

I can smell the smoke of home every day, with the scent of cooking and trees and get on with everything ordinary in life, even arguing with Plato! While my luck holds, that is *almost* good enough for me. But there's still a lot that needs changing in the world too!

Demos himself arrived a bit later than Dad from the Assembly. It was very different from the way he came to the house before. Tigris could tell the difference immediately, because he didn't run away, even if he didn't rush over to be patted either.

For a moment, Demos and Dad stood facing one another in the courtyard.

'I don't agree with you about the treaty, my son,' Dad began, and I wondered what was going to happen next. Was our family trouble about to break out again? 'But I know you are saying what you and lots of others really think and feel – and you spoke well today – I was proud of you, even if I wanted the Assembly to vote the other way.'

Silence hovered, and then Demos answered, in his quieter way of talking that I had first heard at the end of the play: 'It matters a lot to me, Dad, that you think I spoke well. I mean, a *lot* more than whether all those others voted for my view or against. It's . . . it's the most important thing for me . . .'

The peacocks wandered behind us as we stood, the tree ruffled its leaves and you could even imagine, for a few moments, that our ship had come safely into the harbour.

Then a high, quick voice spoke up. It was my little brother Plato, coming out and catching hold of one loose thread of the chat: 'I think if something seems right to a great crowd of citizens in the Assembly, that just shows it's bound to be *wrong*. It's more likely something is true if most of *them* think it's false!'

'Now hang on a minute, Plato!' cried my big brother. 'Then it would be a bad thing to make a good speech to the Assembly . . .'

'Well, I don't think truth is what makes people believe speeches,' Plato shot back, immediately.

I couldn't leave them to it, of course . . .

'Now I think you're both missing the point,' I began. 'You see . . .'

Mum and Dad watched as the ideas bounced around between the three of us, like sunshine and shadows chasing over the stones and grass.

# Things you might wonder about . . .

**YOU:** So how much of that was history?

**ME:** It's a made-up story with some real people from ancient Athens in it, so it's hard to be sure!

**YOU:** OK, so just remind me which of them are the real ones?

**ME:** Well, the two children called Potone and Plato were real. Plato's name was Aristocles, but he was known by the nickname 'Plato' meaning 'broad shoulders'. The children and their mother Perictione lived with their stepfather Pyrilampes after their father Ariston died. As Potone says, they lived in an area of Athens called Collytus, where many of the richest families were. Demos *was* their older stepbrother. Their ages are about what it says, although nobody kept birthdays in the way we do now, so it's not exact. There *was* a famous teacher called Socrates in Athens at the time, and he did act as the person in charge of at least one big trial. The story at the end about the poor woman called Theoris is also true.

**YOU:** And how much of what it says about these people is history?

**ME:** Lots of bits are. Pyrilampes *had* been the Ambassador from Athens to Persia, from where he returned with the famous peacocks. In fact, people from the city were allowed to come and see them once a month, they were so unusual! He also had a golden bowl from Persia. Demos was quite well-known for being poshly dressed and also very good at persuading people, especially in the Assembly. By the way, his name, Demos, was actually the Greek word for 'the people' – it is still there, without the -s, in our word 'democracy', which means 'the rule of the people'. Pyrilampes had given him that name when he was born because he was a close friend of a famous Athenian leader called Pericles, who had the support of the people against his rivals.

**YOU:** What about Potone and Plato?

**ME:** Plato went on to become very famous – and he still is today. As he grew up, he got very interested in 'philosophy', the love of wisdom, which Socrates taught, and after some other teachers, he went and studied with him. Later he wrote many books about ideas. They are unusual in lots of ways, and especially because when you read them, they look like plays, with different characters speaking to one another. Plato is not a character in his own books – usually Socrates is the most important speaker. He often spends a lot of time asking difficult questions which the other people struggle to answer. These characters include other thinkers or philosophers, whose ideas get demolished by Socrates as the talk goes on! Sometimes Socrates gives his own answers, but often he leaves things as puzzles to think about. I guess you can tell from this that Plato in the story is how I imagine the writer of those books might have been when he was growing up.

In some ways the most historical thing in the story is hidden! Quite a few of the actual ideas that they argue about also come from Plato's books. Even though he was a great writer, he didn't trust writing – and that turns up here when young Plato complains about having to learn writing! Plato also worried that plays trick people into getting carried away by stories that aren't much like life! Then he wrote a lot about how we can tell what's true from what's false – which is the main bit of the trial of Tigris – and quite a few of the other ideas in the trial come from his books too. He even had things to say about dogs, and how clever they can be! So, in a sneaky way, you've been reading a lot of Ancient Greek ideas and especially Plato's ideas in this story – and I hope you want to find out more about them, because they're really interesting and important. I wanted to give a bit of a feeling of how Plato makes people *talk* in his own books – with lots of questions and answers. I also think Plato must have been a chatterbox and full of questions or he would never have written his books like that! Even if he lived two thousand, four hundred years ago.

**YOU:** But what about Potone?

**ME:** It's much harder to know about her life, because she left no records. It was a real tragedy how girls and women had much less choice open to them, even if, like her, they came from well-off and important families. We do know she got married and she and her brother Plato lived in houses near each other when they grew up. We also know that her son, called Speusippus, went to learn philosophy from his uncle Plato, and even became the head of his uncle's school for philosophers after Plato got older. Speusippus wrote a lot of books where people talk to each other about ideas too, but none of them have come down to us. It seems from what other people say that he didn't agree with his uncle Plato about lots of these ideas! I think he might have got his interest in thinking and arguing also from his mum, Potone – but that's my idea, not something I can prove. Surely if she let her son go and study with his uncle, she must have been keen on the ideas too. Otherwise, I've tried to *imagine* how

she and her brother Plato might have
talked when they were young – and
what they could have been like – but
again, those are my ideas, even if
they're based on things I've found out.

There's one other side of Potone
herself that is real, in a different way.
All the proverbs that Potone loves, and
uses, are real ancient Greek sayings
turned into English. Proverbs are
interesting because you usually don't
know who started them and some
people nowadays think, as Potone does,
that women have begun many of them.

**YOU:** There's a lot in the story about
Athens having this Assembly. Did that
make it a kind of democracy?

**ME:** You do often hear that Athens
began democracy – well, it was an
ancient Greek word, and it meant that
the people governed themselves, rather
than being governed by a king or by a
small group of powerful rulers. That's
the Assembly in the story. It's sort of
true, but all the citizens who voted
were men, and neither women nor

those who were enslaved had any vote or say. The trials where juries decided who was guilty or innocent went with democracy, because you had to persuade the judges (or you could call them the jury) like you had to try and persuade the Assembly to vote for what you wanted . . . that's if you were allowed to speak at all! Women were sometimes tried in the courts, but the speakers and jury and judges were men.

**YOU:** So, do you think this story *could* have happened then?

**ME:** Hmmm, some of the things in it did happen – the treaty and the play *Peace* written by Aristophanes and acted by Apollodorus were both in the spring of the same year, 421 BCE, and the treaty was actually signed very soon after the performance. The law about violent dogs was real with the bit about the wooden collar too. It was also true that statues could be tried if they fell on someone and squashed them. The trial about magic was real too and it happened just a year or so before. On the family side,

Pyrilampes did go to war and fought at Delium, where he was wounded and Socrates was a bit of a hero. The trial of Tigris, the struggle Potone and Plato have with Demos and Potone's friendship with Niko, are made up, of course, and I guess as with any made-up story it's hard to be sure if anything *could* have happened exactly like that.

If you give any story a sort of happy ending, lots of people will always say it is way too hopeful, perhaps especially given how bad things were for girls and women. Well, I think the end of the story *is* on the hopeful side in some ways, the way it sorts itself out – but then the ending kind of spills over from the comedy in the theatre, so there's something in it that's maybe not so realistic as other parts!

**YOU:** Was *that* really a Greek play? I mean, there aren't funny songs from 'The Wheels on the Bus' or football crowds in it, are there?

**ME:** True, no there aren't! But the *story* with the beetle and Hermes and

190

the pit and the rope and the wedding *is* the plot of *Peace* as they performed it on a spring day two-and-a-half thousand years ago. I've added the songs because the thing with a funny play is that it has to *stay* a bit funny still, or that isn't really how it was – so perhaps you could say the songs are in the spirit of the comedy. The crazy songs do also fit with the real *Peace* in some other ways. It has got lots of altered bits of other plays and poems and sayings and songs in it, which people would have noticed. In this story, it's Apollodorus who adds the songs, as I'm sure actors did add funny things to the comedies. It was performed right before the treaty was signed and surely there must have been arguments and all kinds of shouts and yells in the audience, since people didn't agree!

**YOU:** At least that bit of history ends with peace then, like the play?

**ME:** Ah, well, yes and no, like lots of answers about history! The trouble is that though there was a treaty called the Peace of Nicias, it didn't last for long and the fighting did start again – it went on for many more years. I guess it could be like that in the family story too – trouble has a way of coming back, after we think we've sorted it out. Then again, maybe next time round, we have more idea what to do about it. And eventually there *was* peace between Athens and Sparta.

**YOU:** One way you get a happy ending, the other way it's more worrying.

**ME:** I agree – there's things we can find out, but in the end, we still have to decide about the stories they can make. And there are so many gaps in the facts about the past, that without imagination it's hard to bring it to life. Potone is much more lost to us than Plato – but at least the story reminds you that she did exist, and was a real person, just as much as her famous brother.

# Acknowledgements

I'd like to thank David and Sandra Hopkins for their enlivening and enriching responses to this story as it began to emerge and their continuing support and interest, and Max Saunders for his inexhaustibly patient readings and re-readings and insights. I would also like to thank Eloise Wilson and Chloe Sackur at Andersen Press for their deeply enabling and ever-resourceful work on helping this book become the best version of itself it could be.

# THE
# VIKING
## ATTACK

# JOSH LACEY
ILLUSTRATED BY **GARRY PARSONS**

Discover two sides of history with the Time Travel Twins!

Twins, Scarlett and Tom, are studying the Vikings and Anglo-Saxons at school and they have a homework project to do. When Tom's struggling for inspiration, Grandad comes to the rescue with his time machine. Tom is catapulted onto a Viking long ship and it's not long before he's being told oral tales, fitted out with armour and weapons and is getting ready to attack a Saxon village.

But uh oh, his sister Scarlett has landed in a Saxon village, in a pile of pig poo to be exact. Things seems to be getting better when she befriends the young Alfred the Great, but watch out, Scarlett, there's a Viking ship on its way.

# TIME TRAVEL TWINS

# THE ROMAN

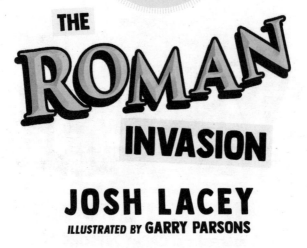

# INVASION

# JOSH LACEY

### ILLUSTRATED BY GARRY PARSONS

Discover two sides of history with the Time Travel Twins!

Twins, Scarlett and Thomas, are learning about the Romans at school. So Grandad uses his time machine to send them back to Roman Britain.

Scarlett finds herself in a Roman camp and is chosen as a slave by the Emperor Claudius's daughter, Antonia. The two become friends and Scarlett sees first hand the glamour and treachery of the Roman court.

Thomas joins a rabble of local kids who hate the Romans. Their leader is a small red-headed girl called Boudicca. Even when the kids are overwhelmed and taken as slaves, Bou hatches another plan to attack the Romans.

Will the twins find each other and escape, or will they both be stuck as Roman slaves for ever?

# HOPE JONES SAVES THE WORLD

Written by
## JOSH LACEY

Illustrated by
## BEATRIZ CASTRO

**SHORTLISTED FOR THE LITTLE REBELS BOOK AWARD**

*My name is Hope Jones. I am ten years old. I am going to save the world.*

Hope Jones' New Year's resolution is to give up plastic, and she's inspiring others to do the same with her website hopejonessavestheworld.com. When she realises her local supermarket seems to stock more unnecessary plastic than food, she makes it her mission to do something about it. She may be just one ten-year-old with a homemade banner, but with enough determination, maybe Hope Jones really can save the world.

'Powerful, inspirational . . . an amusing and engaging story which cannot fail to have a positive impact on the reader'
- *The School Librarian*

# SEASON OF SECRETS

## SALLY NICHOLLS

On a wild and stormy night Molly runs away from her grandparents' house. Her dad has sent her to live there until he Sorts Things Out at home now her mother has passed away. In the howling darkness, Molly sees a desperate figure running for his life from a terrifying midnight hunt. But who is he? Why has he come? And can he heal her heartbreak?

'A stand-out story . . . exciting [and] profound'
**Guardian**

'A wonderful, evocative, lively book'
**Literary Review**

9781839130465

# UNTIL THE ROAD ENDS

## PHIL EARLE

A new novel from the bestselling author of *When the Sky Falls: The Times* Children's Book of the Year, winner of a Books Are My Bag Readers Award, the British Book Award for Children's Fiction and shortlisted for the Carnegie Medal.

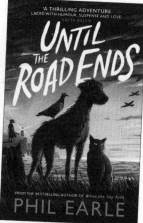

When Peggy saves a stray dog from near-death, a beautiful friendship begins. Peggy and Beau are inseparable: the only thing that can ever come between them is war. Peggy is evacuated to the safety of the coast, but Beau is left behind in the city, where he becomes the most extraordinary and unlikely of war heroes. Night after night, as bombs rain down and communities are destroyed, Beau searches the streets, saving countless families. But then disaster strikes, changing Peggy's life forever. With her parents killed, both she and Beau are left alone, hundreds of miles apart. But Beau has a plan to reunite them at long last . . .

'A heartbreaking story of love and devotion in the midst of war' - *Waterstones*

'This is a thrilling adventure laced with humour, suspense, and love. Just brilliant' - Katya Balen

# DOGS
## Understanding your very
# BEST FRIEND

**Written by Dr John Bradshaw, illustrated by Clare Elsom**

*Learn about the secret life of dogs from pet expert Dr John Bradshaw.*

Join Rusty the terrier as he goes about his day with his family. Discover how Rusty sees and mostly smells the world around him. Rusty uses his amazing nose to recognise his friends – human and dog! – it tells him where to find something tasty to eat and how to get back to his owner.

Find out how Rusty's family make him feel loved and safe, when he meets new people and other dogs, or is left at home alone.

After a day with Rusty, you'll know exactly how to be your dog's best friend.

'Fascinating . . . After you've read the book, you'll know so much about the best ways to keep your dog happy and why they behave the way they do' - Andrea Reece, *LoveReading4Kids*